THE LAST AND
THE FIRST

NINA BERBEROVA

THE LAST AND
THE FIRST

Translated from the Russian
by Marian Schwartz

PUSHKIN PRESS
LONDON

Pushkin Press
71–75 Shelton Street
London WC2H 9JQ

Original title: *Les derniers et les premiers*
© ACTES SUD, 2001
Translation © 2021 Marian Schwartz

The Last and the First was first published serially as *Poslednie i pervye*
in *Sovremennye zapiski* in Paris, 1929, and then as a book
by Jacques Povolozky & Cie in Paris, 1930

First published by Pushkin Press in 2021

ИНСТИТУТ ПЕРЕВОДА

AD VERBUM

Published with the support of the Institute
for Literary Translation (Russia)

1 3 5 7 9 8 6 4 2

ISBN 13: 978-1-78227-697-5

Frontispiece © Heritage Image Partnership Ltd / Alamy Stock Photo

Typeset by Hewer Text UK Ltd, Edinburgh

Printed and bound by TJ Books Limited, Padstow,
Cornwall on Munken Premium White 80gsm

www.pushkinpress.com

THE LAST AND
THE FIRST

TRANSLATOR'S NOTE

B ETWEEN 1917 AND 1920, millions of Russians fled the Revolution and Civil War, hundreds of thousands of them finding refuge in France. By the 1920s, many émigrés feared that the Bolsheviks might prevail and prevent their eventual return, yet they had failed to make new lives for themselves in emigration and faced an uncertain and frightening future. By then, too, Soviet Russia had realized that it needed educated professionals to rebuild the economy and so had initiated a campaign of "returnism," which was aimed in part at luring émigrés back to Russia.

In Berberova's novel, Shaibin and Vasya believe that they are "lasts," representatives of the past who can never adapt to the new era. Torn by competing ideas and emotions, they wonder whether they must inevitably accept defeat and go back to Russia. Others, like Ilya, are "firsts," forging a difficult future in their new environment—raising the contentious issue of assimilation in the process—all the while refusing to abandon Russia and all hope of return.

CHAPTER ONE

ON THE MORNING of 20th September 1928, between nine and ten, three events occurred that set the stage for this tale. Alexei Ivanovich Shaibin, one of its many heroes, turned up at the Gorbatovs'; Vasya, the Gorbatov son, offspring of Stepan Vasilievich and Vera Kirillovna and stepbrother of Ilya Stepanovich, received a letter from Paris, from his friend Adolf Kellerman, with important news about Vasya's father; and finally, a poor wayfarer and his guide arrived at the Gorbatovs' farm in a broad valley of the Vaucluse.

No one knew this man's name. Who was he? What road had led him to his present wanderings? He had passed through here the previous year, in the spring, and he was already known in the surrounding area; at that time he was still sighted and walked alone, an old Astrakhan cap pulled to his eyes, sending up white dust and bowing to those he met. He had spoken with

Ilya and with Vera Kirillovna herself for a long time; he'd drunk, had dinner, and spent the night. But neither Vasya nor his sister Marianna saw the wayfarer the next morning. He had left at dawn, blessing the house, the orchard, and the cowshed where the oxen slept, and the attic where Ilya slept. Later, people said he'd gone west, but more likely he'd gone southwest, past Toulouse, to see the Cossacks who had settled in those parts.

Now he was blind, and that same Astrakhan cap had slipped over his shaggy eyebrows. A dark blue scar ran across his face, and he had no beard growing on his cheeks; you could tell a regimental doctor had once mended his face in haste, slapping together the torn pieces of his no longer young, swarthy skin. He was tall and ominously thin, and his military trousers sported red patches in many places—possibly scraps from someone else's service trousers, but French, trousers that had once known the defense of Verdun. The wayfarer walked with his harsh withered hand resting on the shoulder of his guide, a black-eyed girl of about twelve whose name was Anyuta.

They stopped at the gate and the old man took off his cap. The girl looked over the low stone wall. There she saw an orchard, a vegetable plot, and a house with outbuildings partially hidden by stocky willows. In the silence and cool of the morning, the house stood low, burned by the sun over the long summer, with a north-facing porch and squat asparagus shoots, while farther away, past the dark blue shadow of moribund cypresses, plowed fields spread out, ready for winter crops.

This was a human habitation created not in struggle with nature but at one with it. The sun was already high in the untroubled sky, and birds flew swiftly in its gleam, like short, darting needles sewing through it.

Vasya and Marianna went over to the gate, even though they were up to their ears in work; they pushed back their round straw hats, which were as hard as tin, and their hands were covered in dirt.

"You could have sung something," Marianna said. "Where have you come from?" She began examining Anyuta, her long colorful skirt and the narrow ribbon tied around her head.

The wayfarer made a low, unhurried bow.

"From the Dordogne, gentle lady," he said. "We are on our way south, from the Dordogne to the Siagne River, to hot climes, to see good people, and in the spring back to our own people, for the summer. And there—God will provide. People know us."

Vasya came closer, his face bathed in sweat.

"But what are you going there for?" he asked.

Anyuta gave him a frightened look. Her heart started pounding for fear they would have to leave without seeing the person they'd come to see, for the sake of whom they'd made a detour from the highway, past the river and mill. How can these people ask! How dare they! she thought.

"We walk, my dear boy," the wayfarer replied, "because we're too old and blind to work. We go to good people's homes to eat and have conversations with good people, and we do not complain of our Lord God."

Marianna shrugged lightly and grinned.

"Why do you speak so oddly? We were told you were an educated man, or else a priest."

Anyuta rushed to the old man in despair.

"Granddad, can we go? Granddad?" she whispered, tugging on his sleeve. "Let's go, dear Granddad. We can come some other time!"

The beggar put his hand on her shoulder but did not go where she was pulling him. He took two steps toward the wall, making a deep rut in the road dust with his staff.

"They told you wrong, my good lady," he replied, and his micaceous eyes flashed. "I am no priest. Nor was I a doctor or an engineer. Allow us to sit on your little porch. I know in your part of the world porches always look into the shade, and if Vera Kirillovna can find a little water for us, Anyuta and I would be very grateful."

And he bowed abruptly at the waist.

Marianna opened the gate, and the wayfarer passed between her and Vasya, Anyuta leading him. He walked majestically, without that grim fussiness so often characteristic of the blind. They passed slowly between the vegetable beds toward the house; from time to time the beggar lifted his right hand from Anyuta's thin shoulder and made a fluid cross over the beds, and the house, and the bent pear trees' smeared trunks. A sack hung motionlessly from his shoulder; the sack was military, like his trousers. No one knew this man's name.

Marianna watched him go, grinned again, and leaned over the shoots poking out of the earth.

"Come on, let's go, let's listen," Vasya said, "or does nothing have anything to do with you anymore?"

He wiped his wet face with his sleeve and looked at her expectantly.

"No, it doesn't," Marianna replied reluctantly. "There's nothing for me to hear. But you go on."

Something stirred in Vasya's sleepy face; his gaze slid down Marianna's back, her black gathered skirt, her wooden shoes.

"I've just had a letter from Adolf," he said sullenly. "Has that nothing to do with you?"

Marianna turned her merry, high-cheekboned face toward him.

"You mean he's summoning you?"

"Yes. He writes about Father. Old Kellerman has come and wants a meeting with me. Father's been found, and he has an important post."

Marianna clapped her hands and gave her brother a frightened look.

"Ah, that Gorbatov!" she exclaimed. "He lets us know through Kellerman. He wants to lure you there!"

Vasya sat down beside her and put an arm around his knees.

"It's time for me to go," he said firmly. "Father is calling, demanding that at least one of us return. At first old Kellerman was going to demand Adolf get Ilya, but Adolf told him flat out that was impossible. Whereas I . . . I've been wanting to go there for a whole year, and Adolf has summoned me. He writes that my papers can be in order in two days."

"A whole year!" Marianna said slowly.

"I never tried to pretend otherwise. Mama knows it, and so does Ilya. I just can't here. My path takes me home, to Father, and this is the goal Kellerman and I share." He dropped his head. "I know that Kellerman is trying to get in Father's good graces, but does that matter, Marianna? I might have gone even without this."

"No, you wouldn't!"

"I don't know. It's impossible for me here. Father's working with Kellerman there and despises our settling here. I'm going. I'll have money, I'll have the life I want. I didn't choose this one. And you know, it's essential to me—I mean, roots are absolutely essential."

"Ilya says we should have roots in the air."

"Ilya's always going to say something you don't know how to answer. But there, Father's a big shot. He sent Kellerman to Paris on business and he's going back in a month. You have to understand. I've been waiting a whole year for this, waiting for Gorbatov to turn up and summon me. Adolf has worn me down!"

"He's the one who won you over, and he's the one sending you after your roots. He's a scoundrel, your Adolf, and Gorbatov's a fine one! To lure you away, to tempt you . . . Oh, Vasya, dear Vasya, what an automaton you are, my God! If I were Ilya I would lock you in the attic and go to Paris myself and demand that Kellerman back off. If they don't leave you in peace— someone should lodge a complaint. There's manure to shovel here and you're leaving!"

Vasya was quiet for a moment.

"It's true, Vasya. Let Ilya go to Paris. Wait for him. This is all about your weak will. You're flattered that a passport will be ready in two days, that—don't laugh—that there's a direct train to Negoreloye, I know. Old Kellerman is clearly trying to curry favor with Gorbatov, he's promising to return his sonny boy, promising sonny boy his roots . . . It would be better if Gorbatov went missing altogether, there'd be more left of him. Did Mama really not talk to you?"

"What can Mama say? Anything she's going to say will be less than what she's doing. If, she says, if you don't see what our whole life's been for, I can't help you. If you haven't understood why we're living like this, so be it. Come back when you have. But Gorbatov, she says—him I curse."

Vasya stood up and wrung his hands in anguish.

"Go," Marianna said, bending over. "She's right. You didn't start this, those scoundrels did, and that includes Gorbatov. Go."

Vasya waited, but Marianna didn't straighten up, and he slowly walked away. Dirt stuck to his wooden shoes. He clasped his hands behind his back. He hesitated as to where to go and started uncertainly toward the house. The kitchen door was wide open, Anyuta was sitting in the doorway, and her slender little fingers were sorting through a bunch of dark, dusty grapes. The wayfarer's low, placid voice reached her from the kitchen.

Through her spread fingers Marianna clearly saw which way Vasya had gone. As soon as he disappeared into the kitchen, she jumped up, let down her tucked skirt, wiped her hands on her hem, straightened the hat on her short, thick hair, and ran out of the gate.

There wasn't a soul on the road at that already hot morning hour. The untouched track made by the postman who'd buzzed by here on his bicycle an hour before lay calmly in the dust. The black fields and the bands of meadows that had been mowed for a third time were empty and scentless, as they are in the autumn. Marianna ran tentatively at first and then faster and faster. When she finally reached the main road, she shot off like an arrow down the dismal old boundary path, her heavy strapped wooden shoes pounding. She flew past the stubble field and skirted the old farm; a dog yelped and wet linens rustled in the wind. She ran as far as the grove and stopped. Something cracked in the branches.

"Gabriel!" she called quietly.

Somewhere cows were moving, their bells tinkling, and the young oaks smelled of the Provençal valleys' eternal freshness.

"Gabriel," Marianna repeated, trying not to breathe too loudly or step too heavily. Just then she saw a cap on the ground. Gabriel was asleep, his head resting on the back wheel of his bicycle. Marianna flung herself at him and shouted right in his ear—"Gabriel!"—so that he started, swept his arm around her neck, and pulled her toward him. He smelled of pine needles and clabber, and she kissed him hard.

His apron, draped over one shoulder, was, as usual, covered in blood spots, and his cowlick was pomaded down. Marianna was crazy about his tiny teeth and early mustache, and she sat on a hummock to take it all in. Excitement and happiness had transformed her face.

"What did your father say?" she asked in French, with a faint Provençal accent, as she always spoke, as her neighbors had taught her. "Did you talk to him?"

"He said yes," Gabriel replied, glancing slyly at her. "He said yes, but he asked who exactly I was in love with, you or Ilya."

Marianna blushed.

"What did you say?"

"Botheration! With you! Then he started laughing and said that according to his information I was in love with Ilya, at least that's what people in town said, and just about me."

"So he said yes?" Marianna repeated, gasping.

"Not right off, don't imagine that. First he asked whether I really wanted to go from shopkeeper to peasant. Then I told him I wanted to be a landowner."

"Is that so! You were able to put it that well?"

"Well, yes. I explained I was going into business with Ilya, that we were thinking about the future. Yes, he said, you mean the free farms on the other side of Saint-Didier and the canning factory? Ilya told me about them. But did he really decide to sow wheat this year anyway? After all, it's much less profitable than, say, raising silkworms or even growing strawberries. Wait, I told him. Ilya's already thought about strawberries, but it's a secret, and besides, he'd been thinking about asparagus. But wheat, as he puts it, for him, it's a matter of conviction, wheat is essential. My father laughed again. I know all your secrets. Ilya tells me them himself. Why don't you tell me instead what you think about her being a foreigner? I could tell from his sniff that he'd discussed that with Ilya. What do you think yourself, Papa? I asked, because I had no idea what to say. And then he started rambling so that I didn't understand half of it. Turns out, he wanted to say that in our case it doesn't matter, but if I stayed at the shop you would have a bad time of it. Or some other nonsense. 'La terre? La terre?' he kept saying. 'C'est tout autre chose.' But right then Lucie wheeled Mama in, and I'd barely managed to tell him that Ilya was going to start building a new cowshed soon when everyone started bellowing, Mama blessed me, and Lucie asked whether she could do something with the asparagus too. And I think I bellowed like a pig too."

"How muddled you tell it!" Marianna threw up her hands. "I can't make head or tail of anything."

"There's nothing more to tell."

"Well then, tell it one more time."

Gabriel crept toward her, put his arms around her shoulders, and smothered her with kisses.

"Do you love me?" he asked.

"I do," she replied.

"Now you ask," he said, twirling her hat in his hands.

"There's nothing to ask. I already know."

"What do you know?"

"That you do."

"Do what?"

"Love me."

"Yes, and then Ilya. But you more, because kissing you is so sweet."

Marianna lowered her head. Her heart was pounding.

"Well then, kiss me," she said.

He embraced her again.

"What do you think? How will it all be?" she whispered.

"I think it will all be good." He rocked her, his arms firmly around her shoulders. "When will you come?"

"Tomorrow."

"Come at this same time, no later. On Sunday my father's going to go see your mother after church. You tell her."

"She already knows everything."

"Then tell Ilya that on Saturday after dinner I'm coming to saw planks so he should leave the saw in the yard for me if he goes away."

"He's probably going to Paris."

"Paris! Now that's splendid."

"He may even go tomorrow, but he'll be back in a few days. He has business there."

"Well, give him my regards."

"All right."

"You won't forget?"

"No."

"And tell him that he's all anyone in town is talking about."

"What are they saying?"

"All sorts of things. That ten years from now he'll be the top man here."

"Ten years!" A shadow crossed Marianna's face. "Not another word about that."

Gabriel hugged her again, cheerfully and roughly, and hopped on his bicycle. There was a basket tied to the bars and something wrapped in a newspaper bobbing around in it.

"I'm delivering a roast to the miller's wife," he explained, and he cocked his cap back on his head. "Two and a half pounds of filet. She has guests coming. Goodbye!" And he rode over the pine needles to the edge of the forest.

Marianna shouted and waved, ran back down the boundary path, over the stubble-field, past the old farm, and down the highway and road, but not in the same kind of hurry now, as if deep in thought. One time she stopped and gazed into the distance. She thought she saw a black dot moving in the field where the willows bristled, extending their branches into the sky's blue clarity.

"Ilyusha!" she shouted as loudly as she could, but no one answered and the dot disappeared. She stood for a minute. The sun spread across the sky, and she smelled the dry earth; a thousand thoughts raced inside her, awful, joyful. She ran on farther, not stopping now until she reached the kitchen door.

The beggar was sitting at the table with his back to the window and his hands palm down on the coarse tablecloth. He'd just finished eating, his dishes had been cleared, and the bread and cheese were still on the table. Anyuta was sitting on the small bench by the door, propping herself up on both arms, occasionally glancing out of the window, as if expecting someone. Vera Kirillovna Gorbatova was sitting opposite the visitor, her arms folded and her head tilted very slightly, and listening.

She was a full forty years old. An early marriage, children, a strong secret passion, and Russia's demise had made of her what she had become. Tall and dark-haired, with dark gray eyes (on Marianna, these same eyes were burdened by her father's shaggy eyebrows, while on Vasya they had faded to his father's muddy blue), Vera Kirillovna was still beautiful. There wasn't a single gray hair in her simple, smooth coiffure; but after ten years of constant, hard, and brutal work, her hands had lost their suppleness and gentle color and that special "maternal" smell she'd exuded in her youth. It was not her forbidden passion that had stolen this inexplicable fragrance; labor, not women's labor but human labor and now the black Provençal earth, had stolen from her soft hands the youth her body still retained in full. On Sundays, in town, many gave her admiring looks when she passed in her black pleated cotton dress, straw hat, and city shoes and stockings, when she walked down the main street past the tobacco shop, the hairdresser's, the butcher's and the other, horsemeat, butcher's, accompanied by a tall, fair-haired young man wearing a suit tailor-made somewhere else, with a ruddy face, blue eyes, broad shoulders, and long arms. On Sundays, oh, many watched her, admiring her and saying, "Look, there goes the Russian woman from the farm. She's handsome and young. That young man is her stepson, but she has grown children of her own. Her daughter's engaged to the butcher's son, not that one, the other, the horsemeat one, and her son will soon be twenty, he's educated and polite, and he resembles her in the face."

Many would bow to her, recognizing her, and she would smile at them with her eyes, and the fair-haired young man would doff his hat, or simply carry it, and the quiet Sunday breeze would blow across his clear face.

Vera Kirillovna was sitting at the table wearing a full apron, her hands folded, listening to the wayfarer. The kitchen shutters were half open, and a ray of light fell through the window and onto the hearth, benches, cupboard, and scrubbed utensils, and a small, unsealed barrel of tomatoes. Steam rose over the stove, linens boiled in a tall vat, and the sweet smell of turnips and leeks escaped a pot lid. The beggar was talking, and he seemed to turn his dark, blind face with its sickly, uneven beard most eagerly of all toward Vasya, who was standing by the lintel. A cigarette stuck to his lip and an early furrow between his eyebrows, Vasya couldn't help but catch this cold, senseless gaze that didn't mesh with the blind man's sad voice.

"May God bless you, my dear friends. I should be back by Easter. I won't forget your kindness and will stop by on my final journey to say goodbye. I won't last the spring. It's time for me to go to my long rest, a repose without tears. Vera Kirillovna, my last concern in this life is Anyuta. This isn't the time to say who she is or where she comes from, and it's too soon to entrust her to anyone. Let her go with me and learn how Russian people live, in Old Testament labor and Christian thought. God bless us and have mercy upon us!"

He crossed himself.

"For you, Vera Kirillovna, a special prayer to God. Last spring I didn't expect you would become so firmly established in your life, be worn so smooth. I'd like to sing you a song they sing in the Dordogne. It would please you. It's as though it were a song just for you."

"Sing it," Marianna said, sitting down beside Anyuta.

"For you, for you, my dear young lady, and for you, my dear boy." The old man turned to Vasya. "This song gives you the answer, the answer most understandable for Russian people, the most modest. Hold on, it says, hold on, Russian man! . . . I'll tell you in all confidence, I think the song is about Ilya Stepanovich."

Vasya grinned.

"Let's hear," he said, crossing his arms at his chest.

That very moment, someone's shadow passed across the window, someone's not-too-quickly-stepping shadow, a man in a brimmed hat, tall but round-shouldered, and there was something wrong with his gait. Vera Kirillovna looked up. The stranger's steps were heard on the porch behind Marianna. It was definitely a man with an irregular, even weary gait. It was Alexei Ivanovich Shaibin, arrived from Africa.

His pale face was covered in light perspiration, and everything about him said that he had come from town on foot and had been traveling for more than a day.

"Alyosha!" Vera Kirillovna exclaimed, rising from the table. "My God, Alyosha!"

"Hello," Shaibin said, removing his hat and revealing a half-gray head. "It just so happened that I arrived earlier than I'd intended."

Silence fell. Anyuta dashed to the beggar in fright. Vera Kirillovna was still standing by the table. She felt Vasya's and Marianna's gaze—neither one could keep their eyes off her at that moment. A certain amount of time passed, and Shaibin was still standing in the doorway. Then, in the same instant, they rushed toward each other. He grabbed her hands and clung to them, and she with a sudden, cautious softness meekly and gently kissed his temple.

"Who is it?" the blind man said suddenly, standing.

Marianna, who was closest to the old man, whispered the new arrival's name to him. The beggar's head reared back, and he found Anyuta's shoulder with his hand; frightened and sad, she pressed close to him.

"Where are you going?" Vasya suddenly asked loudly and firmly. "Where? You wanted to sing." He took two steps. His eyes were flashing. "You have to sing, that's what you wanted. I know that's why you came. Marianna, don't let him go. He has to sing." Vasya was agitated. Everyone noticed.

Anyuta rushed for the doorway.

"On our way back, Vasily Stepanovich, my friend, right now your family has other concerns. After a time we'll pass through your parts to summer in the Dordogne and then we'll keep our promise, and we'll have a lot to talk about, and Ilya Stepanovich and I will meet."

Marianna stepped away from the door.

"After a time!" Vasya shouted. "But so much will have happened by then! Time doesn't pass for us the way it does for you."

But the beggar was walking away.

"Don't be alarmed. I've come to you at the wrong time. In the name of the Father, the Son, and the Holy Spirit."

The dry autumn grasses were fragrant; pears, ruddy and rough, swung above Anyuta's head.

"He's not here, Granddad," she whispered without turning around. "Granddad, it was wrong to come, wrong to get mixed up in this. You didn't get to see Ilya Stepanovich, Granddad."

The road's soft dust lay before them. Silently, they started down along the walls. Here Marianna had run, here in the morning the postman had passed with the fat letter in his leather sack, here Alexei Ivanovich Shaibin had walked from the station.

And at that very same time Ilya Gorbatov caught up with them.

He came running out from somewhere past the vegetable plot. Hopping the wall, he took off toward the road. He had a face overgrown with a light fuzz, and deep blue eyes, the kind children have, eyes that had driven young women from all over the district mad. "Stop!" he shouted. "Hey! Stop!"

The wayfarer stopped and Ilya pressed his hand with both of his.

"My dear, dear man. Let me hold you to my heart," the blind man exclaimed. "I can't see you anymore, my sweet Ilyusha. I'm old and blind now. And I don't have long to live. The bullets in me hurt."

Stunned, Ilya silently faced the old man.

"We're leaving, we're in a hurry, I have my reasons. Here's the girl I wrote you about. Anyuta, just look, he chased us down, our Ilyusha. That means we weren't wrong to have turned off!"

"But where are you going?" Ilya exclaimed, when he realized what was happening. "Can you really not stay for a day? Has Vera Kirillovna even seen you?"

"Vera Kirillovna has a visitor. That's why we left."

"What kind of visitor? From where?"

"Alexei Ivanovich Shaibin. Four years ago in Paris I had occasion to know him."

"Shaibin's come!" Ilya exclaimed, increasingly agitated. "Wait . . . Did she not say anything to you about a letter?"

"No, dear friend, she didn't. She promised to but clearly never got to it."

Ilya caught the beggar by the sleeve.

"I beg of you. Go back. You don't even know what's been happening with us. True, tomorrow I have to go to Paris. Gorbatov's turned up and he's trying to lure Vasya back."

The wayfarer quietly shook his head and put his hand on Anyuta's shoulder.

"We can't," he said solemnly and weightily. "Neither of us can. We simply can't, with Alexei Shaibin."

Ilya ran his hand over his face and then noticed Anyuta as if for the first time.

"Hello, little girl," he said. "Was it you who wrote to me?"

Anyuta silently lowered her head. She was so worked up, she couldn't answer.

"Well then, are you satisfied now?" he asked again. She raised her dark, shining eyes to him.

"Yes," she said, "but Granddad is going to die soon, and then I'm going to work."

The beggar stroked Anyuta's head.

"When I die, Ilyusha, Anyuta will make her way to you," he said contemplatively. "Only don't you give her to anyone."

Ilya didn't dare ask what those words meant.

"So Gorbatov has turned up," the wayfarer continued. "Fight him, fight for your brother. You're smart,

Ilyusha. In the Dordogne your name walks among us in glory."

Ilya blushed.

"There's a song going around there about you. Come spring, I'll sing it. Give Vera Kirillovna my regards. And what of your sister?"

"She's marrying a Frenchman."

"Well? Will they be on the land?"

"Yes."

"Then that's fine. God's blessing, the land is all one.—Protect your brother," the wayfarer said again. "Shaibin prevented me, I would have sung for him. He's pleased to have come into play, that's evident. He fears his fate."

"Many people fear their fate," Ilya said. "They're terrified by our Russian life."

Suddenly agitated, Ilya leaned toward the beggar.

"I cannot forgive Gorbatov," he said in anguish. "I cannot and do not want to forgive the past or the present."

The wayfarer's face immediately became stern, his nose sharpened, and his dark eyelids fluttered over his blind eyes.

"So don't," he whispered, barely audibly. "You don't have to. Be rigorous. Not everything can be forgiven."

Ilya had never seen him like that. Anyuta looked fearfully at them both.

"What are you afraid of, little girl?" Ilya said, and a lightness filled his heart. "Don't be afraid of our conversations."

"She's timid"—and the sternness still did not leave his face. "She's the one they wrote to you about—the orphan."

They embraced and the beggar went his way. The sun was hot and vivid; the earth bleak and quiet. A visitor from Africa, he said to himself, a formerly marvelous person—and a strange alarm passed through his heart when he recalled Shaibin's face glimpsed out of the train car window in Moscow four years before.

CHAPTER TWO

THERE WAS A time—though few remember it— when the broad valley between the three old towns, one of which we call Saint-Didier, there was a time when this valley, like many other places in the district actually, went for a song. In 1907, for instance, there weren't enough working hands on the land in northern Provence. During those years, people paid for a hectare two-thirds of its actual value—three hundred francs—while at the same time, next door, in the direction of M., a hectare yielded fifteen hundred, even two thousand in income a year. Had they planted too many potatoes and beets then? First to raise this important question were the local newspapers, followed by the society of lovers of agriculture in the depart-ment of Vaucluse, followed by the livestock society and the union of Provençal winemakers. Knowledgeable people, in books published for this express purpose, drew the attention of both the owners of the land and the people leasing the land to the half-abandoned valley's exceptionally advantageous location. They wrote about its marvelous climate, about its moisture, rare for those parts, about the degraded role the world had assigned to potatoes and beets. Where we now observe one of the most abundant corners of Provence, where a special, highly profitable industry has flourished right before our eyes—an asparagus canning factory—in 1907 there was nothing to gladden us. Knowledgeable people drew readers' attention in books to the following opportunities:

grapes,
tobacco,
olives,
silk moths,
truffles,
strawberries,
perfume,
asparagus,
fruits,
honey,
timber,
livestock,
cheese,
oats, and
wheat.

All this had long been known to the happy inhabitants on the far side of M.

And now the land had suddenly gone up in value. Members of the agronomical society had come from the district. The part of the valley closer to P. went swiftly and steadily into asparagus of three types, Hanover, Dutch, and green Vaucluse, the land (not a small area) was plowed, fertilizer was brought in, and seedlings were planted that had been ordered in advance from a nursery near Tarascon. They were planted in narrow trenches no more than forty centimeters wide and deep. A year later, the first shoots appeared—and the stalks were chopped down and the land plowed under. The third year, after tilling by horse in the month of March, they picked the first harvest. By this time the canning factory was ready.

Farms were settled around Saint-Didier, fields sowed, silk moths cultivated.

That we began the history of this valley in 1907 is no accident. That was the year Vera Kirillovna married Stepan Vasilievich Gorbatov, who just four months before had buried his first wife, a Siberian, and was living with his young son Ilya in a private home on the Vyborg side of Petersburg.

Stepan Vasilievich was neither young nor old; he was a turn-of-the-century man. In 1907, when Vera

Kirillovna was twenty, he was thirty-five. Was he a Petersburger in the sense that word has taken on for us now? Yes and no. He was a Petersburger from the Vyborg side, he lived for money and business involving money and despite his obscure background had a large fur business, trading primarily with foreign countries. There were probably wholesalers on the rue de Rivoli now who remembered Gorbatov and his excellent pelts from before the war.

No one anywhere had ever heard of Vera Kirillovna.

Having given Gorbatov her delicate hand and maidenly heart, she broke all the ties that bound her to her former life in one fell swoop—the majesty of dreary Vasilievsky Island, where everything she had once held singularly dear to her heart remained: the lovely building of the Bestuzhev Courses, where in the deserted corridors her heart beat like a swallow at the approach of Nikolai Ivanovich Lazarevsky; and the small home of her father, a teacher at the Nasonova school, the home she darted out of the way young Russian women were darting out at the time—to marry an official, a merchant, a court official . . .

Vasya was born two years after her marriage and Marianna a year before the war. But from the first day, Vera Kirillovna knew no greater joy than knowing and loving Ilya. Her heart retained great powers that never failed her for a moment. She and Ilya learned to love Gorbatov's deceased wife, the Siberian, about whom no one knew very much—who she was, what she'd died from—and of whom a vague but bright memory was preserved in the house on the Vyborg side.

All ties to her maidenly life had been broken by the time Alexei Ivanovich Shaibin showed up in Petersburg. Even before, he had occasionally come from Moscow, where he was finishing university, but now he had moved here for good. He had several connections in Petersburg and was preparing to enter government service.

Late in the evening, on his first day back, he stopped his cab at the door of the wooden house. He had two wedding rings in his pocket. He was led into a crowded dining room that smelled of old tobacco and cabbage. "What? She's married? She has two children?" He left without closing the door. An October wind, raw and dreary, burst into the house, fluttered the curtains, and touched the pages of the pupils' notebooks. The old teacher coughed.

Alexei Ivanovich Shaibin seemed terribly ridiculous even to himself. He threw the rings in the Neva, did some serious drinking, and returned to the furnished rooms on Troitskaya where he had the good fortune to be staying. The next morning he wrote a brief note to Vera Kirillovna asking to meet. She went to see him, and the floor attendant showed her the way. She had loved many in her life: she had loved her father, she loved Vasya and Marianna, she loved Ilyusha and Ilyusha's deceased mother. The one man she had never loved at all was Stepan Vasilievich Gorbatov.

Alexei Ivanovich and Vera Kirillovna spent a year in continual intimacy—and then war broke out. Shaibin left for the Caucasus front and for a long time did not answer her letters; Vera Kirillovna came into Gorbatov's undivided possession.

This period of long, lonely waiting for letters, news, and visits had slipped from Vera Kirillovna's memory, crowded out by 1917 and subsequent events. In 1917, Shaibin returned half-crippled. Gorbatov lost everything, and Vera Kirillovna and the children left him to go to Moscow with Shaibin. They spent three months in the same mysterious, renewed intimacy, and then he disappeared again, as he had three years before, and again cast about from one obscure Russian front to another, caught his breath in provincial corners of raging Russia, was, people said, even married once, and finally, in 1924, showed up in Moscow, a few days before Vera Kirillovna was to go abroad. Now she had a completely different, sincere, tormented love and memories, taught by privations and fear. Ilya had turned twenty. Neither he nor she had heard anything from Gorbatov in five years.

Shaibin stood hatless alongside the train car. It was late autumn. Vasya and Marianna were playing in the window. They had to be taught something, clothed and shod. What had the Russian hurricane done to Alexei Ivanovich's weak heart? Had it really managed to drive out his passion for this woman, so many times abandoned, a woman he could not forget? There he stood, silently parting with her yet again. The train whistled; the train began to move. Then he asked, already in motion:

"Where can I find you . . . if . . ."

He had never asked a question like that. She replied amiably, paling a little:

"Paris . . . or no, I don't know. Ilya will decide." And now, four years later, Shaibin had showed up at the farm, direct from Africa.

Marianna walked up to him, flushed from the heat of the burner: she had been stirring the linens and steam from the vat had escaped toward the ceiling.

"Alexei Ivanovich," she said, "is it true you've come to stay with us for good? I ask because we have an awful lot of work and Vasya wants to bolt."

Vasya looked away and Shaibin became flustered.

"I haven't thought that far yet. I haven't decided. Is Vasya leaving?"

"Perhaps you don't know the terms?"

"The most humane conditions. But the life, the life itself! . . . Anyone who can bear it, honor and glory to him; for others, it's too much."

"Did you hear about Gorbatov?" Marianna said again. "News has come from that world, he runs a trust."

Shaibin glanced at Vera Kirillovna, who called him over to the doorway.

"It's not him you're running off to, is it?" Shaibin asked, turning toward Vasya.

Vasya didn't answer. Shaibin stood in the middle of the kitchen for a moment and then quickly, or as quickly as his slight limp allowed, went into Vera Kirillovna's room. The door shut behind him.

In that spacious country room, Shaibin instantly felt the unique, sweet, inexpressible excitement that overtakes you when you're left alone with a woman you once loved madly and fervently and with whom nothing can ever be repeated. Shaibin knew a lot about himself. You might even say that, as a man of a certain generation, he knew almost everything about himself. Like many of them, he knew how to be his own shadow a little: to revive the past in a dream, to move with the present, to find in the cruelty of despair a sensuality accessible to many who, like him, had been thrown out of joint fifteen years before and all these years had burned, not lived, between ecstasies and curses. He knew that neither the duality of soul that had tortured him so sweetly his entire life nor his eternal sobriety amid the most suffocating intoxication distinguished him from the people who shared his destiny, and little by little pride had ceded its place in him to a permanent awareness of mistakes made.

Shaibin experienced these first moments alone with Vera Kirillovna like a great and undeserved joy that he wished he could extend but saw no longer depended on him alone. He walked up to Vera Kirillovna and with a necessary but wholly undaunted confidence took her hands and squeezed them. These were the same hands from which he had once wrested a unique, maternal serenity.

"Well, do with me what you will, do with me what you will," he repeated, and he felt like throwing himself unabashedly at her feet. "I don't think I can be the master of my own life anymore. Teach me to live the way you live. Will you teach me what to do? . . . I abandoned Africa over your letter, but you don't know everything. I must go to Paris . . . Oh, Vera, if only you could look inside me the way you used to!"

"I don't think I could ever do that, Alyosha."

"Don't take your hands away. You summoned me, so do with me what you will, it's up to you. Tell me now, what do you think of me and why did you write?"

"I wrote," Vera Kirillovna began, extricating her hands from Shaibin's hot hands, "to propose that you live with us. I wanted you to quit the Foreign Legion. Really, Alyosha, after loving yourself your whole life the way you did, you ended up in one of the most terrible places a Russian could, and there are so many terrible places! You heard me, you understood me, right? I'm inviting you to live here, with us. You can stay as long as you like and work as much as you can. Ilya is starting a major business—as long as we're not in Russia, our place is on the land. You'll retain your freedom. I know the first year everything will seem very hard and very boring . . . But your future is in joining together with other people like you. Save yourself. That's all I'm asking."

Shaibin listened to her, seated on Marianna's bed. The room smelled of lavender from a partially shut old bureau drawer.

"I think you truly do want to teach me something," he said. "But your letters . . . I have to warn you that this wasn't the only reason I came to France."

Vera Kirillovna clenched her hands under her apron.

"Alyosha, don't worry, I do know, you think I summoned you here to—how hard it is for me after all to say that old word!—to love you again. No, that's not true. Don't trust that treacherous thought. Right now I'm making you an offer." She clenched her hands even harder. "Stay and work with us. That I'm the same woman you knew and loved is beside the point here."

"You're promising me heaven on earth straight away and don't even want to know whether I want heaven," Shaibin said slowly. "I did think I'd find you different, I mean, the way you were, and you talking about serenity and freedom . . ."

"You expected me to still love you, Alyosha," she said quietly, meeting his eyes. "You were mistaken."

Neither said a word for a minute.

"You haven't changed," Vera Kirillovna said. "You keep complicating your life, relentlessly. I don't know what your thoughts were an hour ago. Maybe you were hoping I'd start offering myself to you—just so you could reject me. Or—don't interrupt!—you were expecting me to ask you first about why you have to go to Paris and were getting ready to torment me with riddles. You have to realize that I'm making you this offer bravely and in a completely new way and I want you to agree to save yourself."

"From what?"

"From perishing, Alyosha."

"Why, when Russia has perished?"

"But aren't you Russia?"

Shaibin raised his head.

"You have me running in circles. I need time to think this through and sort it out," he said harshly. "Yes, I am Russia, and I'm drowning alongside her."

"Then hold on. Russia is immortal, Russia will surface, and then where will you be?"

Vera Kirillovna was upset. Surprised, Shaibin listened to her gentle, vibrant voice.

"You're luring me to this heaven on earth with incredible skill," he said. "I suspected you'd want to show me some path, but I didn't anticipate the path would be so short. It takes great strength, Vera, not to do it, not to just let my heart soften and desire the lap of nature. But where does anyone get that strength?"

He thought about that for a minute.

"What power the past has over us!" he said. "What's most terrible is that we're too weak to fight its power, and little by little we're even starting to find a certain sweetness in it, to love it. Right, Vera?"

"Yes."

"So you do agree with me about something. Does that mean you love what there was?"

"What there was," Vera Kirillovna replied quietly, "was my whole life."

"Repeat that."

"You're my whole life?"

Shaibin felt the familiar sense of an almost physical splitting. He couldn't control himself, he started hearing voices audible to him alone. Throw yourself at her feet! passed through him like a breath. Run! Run! came a shout from somewhere inside him. She's casting her spell over you!

Shaibin stood up and took two steps to calm his pounding heart.

"I'll tell you my decision tomorrow," he said without looking at her. "If only you knew how essential it is that I go to Paris!"

Vera Kirillovna said nothing.

"You won't ask why? You always were like that. I'll tell you myself. I have to go because I'm not expected there, not wanted, not loved. You're not wrong. I haven't changed, yes, yes, I'm the same as before, I'm the same man. And now you're bringing me back from death so that I can go to my humiliation and of course my total unfreedom."

"They'll remember Vasya there at least?" Vera Kirillovna asked.

"Remember him? Yes, they will. That's the only thing I know for certain." Shaibin suddenly smiled helplessly. "I've received three letters that make it clear I've been replaced at the very least."

Vera Kirillovna stood up.

"You know, Alyosha, you don't have to wait for tomorrow to answer," she said. "Of course you're not going to stay. Ilya is going to Paris tomorrow, and you and he will go together."

Shaibin ran his hand across his face.

"Tomorrow? Yes, fine, I'll go tomorrow," he repeated. "Thank you. With Ilya? Now that's a little odd, but oh well, all right. It may even be good. You know, I haven't seen her in a long time, since I was in Paris. I arrived when you'd just left for the South. Haven't you noticed, Vera, for some reason I'm always a little bit late? . . . I met her by chance. God knows what she'd been doing. But she had a sister. I came to love her sister. She was married and she had a daughter . . . I didn't know what action to take and left. Maybe she didn't care, or maybe she did, but something terrible happened to that sister: she took poison."

Shaibin sat down quietly, barely getting the last words out. His eyes closed.

"I'm tired from my journey, Vera." He swayed suddenly. "I've begun to tire amazingly quickly. Not only that, I'm a coward. The husband of the one who poisoned herself died just two months ago. Before that I didn't dare return."

He found it difficult to speak. His face, slightly effeminate, gentle and dry, darkened slightly.

"Are you unwell?" Vera Kirillovna asked, reaching out to touch his trembling hands.

"No, it's nothing," he replied. "But what happened to the little girl, her daughter? And then I want to see the other one, you see, the one of God knows what virtue. I love her."

He took Vera Kirillovna's hand and pressed it to his eyes. A minute passed and Vera Kirillovna slowly leaned toward him. Her lips brushed his temple. Shaibin didn't move a muscle. Before she could straighten up, Ilya walked into the room.

Shaibin opened his eyes and dropped Vera Kirillovna's hand, but remained sitting.

"Hello, Alexei Ivanovich," Ilya said. "So here we meet again."

Shaibin's face jerked into a smile, his eyes flashed, and he squeezed the hand Ilya held out to him hard.

"Hello," he said, and it was evident he could barely

control himself. "Well, how are you? What nice things is Anna Martynovna writing you?"

Ilya's face turned dark red and he took a clumsy step back.

"You know Nyusha?" he whispered. Vera Kirillovna looked at them both. Shaibin stood up.

"Do I know her? Yes. I know you too, through her . . . But I think it's time to eat?"

Ilya stood stock-still in the doorway. Shaibin walked up to him, as in a dream, moved him aside, and went out of the door and into the kitchen.

The table was set for three; neither Vasya nor Marianna was there. Shaibin sat down first, his back to the window, in what seemed to him the proprietary, fitting place of honor. He was served greasy meat soup and a hunk of bread. Ilya sat down opposite. There was a large pot with boiled greens in the middle of the table. Vera Kirillovna stood up and served them.

The table, scraped clean by Marianna that morning, had the damp smell of clean wood. An old Paris newspaper had been spread on the low little kitchen cupboard; the paper had yellowed with age and the familiar words Ilya glimpsed had faded. That newspaper had once written about him too—just that, mentioned his name in a certain matter. It was H., writing about the colony in the Basses-Pyrénées.

Ilya sprinkled coarse salt on his bread. His teeth, a little dull at the edges, were white and gleamed in his tan-darkened face, and his dusty hair was fair and poked out in all directions. He was wearing a linen shirt and wide trousers rolled up, like his sleeves. He wore green canvas shoes.

Ilya ate in a leisurely way. Not that he lived in a leisurely way in general—no, that could not be said of him—but life and work demanded his constant, although quite unconscious, observance of a few rules: he ate in a leisurely fashion and slept very soundly, but when he had to think, as now for instance, his face changed a little, and it was hard to say from the outside where exactly the change lay—in his set mouth, in his darkened eyes, or in his broad, smooth forehead, which betrayed Ilya's youth.

They were silent for a long time, sensing that each was thinking about the other, both tormented by doubts. Oh, quite different doubts, and even tormented differently—after all the two of them were so different! Shaibin was a soul on the threshold of his own perpetual hell, experiencing a kind of bliss even from the questions rending his mind. Ilya's soul had stiffened over one single mystery, as if over an open book where not a single symbol was comprehensible to him. Heedless of all shame, bereft of any sense of self-preservation,

Shaibin looked at Ilya as if his outward appearance might hold the clue he sought. Here he is, this first among firsts, was what occurred to him. The first to step away from us, away from our era and into another to which we have no admission. The first of those who are living differently than we ever did. It ended with us and begins with them. Between us lies a chasm between two eras. Whether they are better than us or worse, others will decide . . . Time was torn asunder, no one managed to track the moment this happened, and we ended up here, on one side of the chasm, while they are there, on the other. Here he is in front of me, here are his eyes, shoulders, hands, voice . . . If only I could open him up and see what's there inside, open him up for a second and then slam him shut, just so I knew for certain . . . Oh, I would happily give more than a year of life for this. And it's with him that I'm going to Paris tomorrow? Incredible! I'm going to spend twelve straight hours alone with him—but isn't that frightening? What if, out of the blue, without waiting for me to ask, he tells me something that makes everything clear to me? No, no, I think it's better not knowing anything and doubting like this (are these the last days?), the way I doubted this whole year. Better to prolong those doubts and not rush fate, not violate this secret. My God, is it really in his hands?

So Shaibin thought, while Ilya sat there as though over an open book, unable to decipher what was written. This man knew Nyusha, he was the African she'd written so much about without ever naming him. But what bound them? What kind of man was he? He was a "last," as Nyusha put it. The beggar on the road had said something harsh about him. More than once, Vera Kirillovna had called him a "formerly marvelous person." And he knew Nyusha. Part of her life, sad and cunning, cracked open for Ilya, but he could not find the full answer to his conjectures.

"Are you content, Ilya?" Shaibin asked, propping himself up on his arm. "I mean, are you content with this life of yours?"

"Yes," Ilya replied. "Did Mama suggest you stay?"

"I can't stay," Shaibin said. "Not yet. You hear me, Vera? I said 'yet.' But Ilya, are you really coping with all this hard labor? You'll forgive me if I ask the stupidest, most mundane question?"

"I work and Marianna works—she no worse than any man. This summer we had a laborer, Terenty Fedotov, but he went his own way, joined some other Russians, and started his own farm. We'll have Gabriel—that's Marianna's fiancé—and if Vasya leaves, I'll find people in the colony."

"The colony?"

"Yes, in the Basses-Pyrénées. There are a lot of us there. Not only that, I'm in contact with an entire group in Paris. A good forty people there want to set up not far from here."

"But the work itself?"

"You mean you want to know whether it's hard? Yes, very. Especially the first year."

"You've been here three years?"

"Mama and the children have been here three years. I arrived six months before and worked as a hand on a farm not far from here and learned a few things. It's especially important to know the trades. At first glance you think, what good are they? But in fact it helps a lot, otherwise you have to bother your neighbors over every little thing. I worked as a farm-hand for six months and learned a lot, and I found people in town who were sympathetic to Russians settling here. Someone in Saint-Didier is trying right now to get not only free farms but also forests leased. You can see over there"—Ilya pointed out the window—"the surveyors are out working now. Last spring we managed to switch to tenancy, which is of course a completely different thing from share-cropping. You're nearly a full owner, you're not dependent on anyone, you're not afraid of any deadlines, and you don't have to reckon with an owner. People here are happy to lease land too, and for long terms.

". . . It's hard, of course. And before starting anything, you have a lot to learn: find out when the planting season is, and figure out what exactly to sow and how, and learn to plow with oxen if you don't know how, and even learn how to harness and feed them. There are so many different branches of agriculture here, but we Russians may be better suited to major crops, we're afraid of truffles, olives, and grapes. That's what people say about us, that we're afraid of grapes, and they laugh at us a little. People here raise special draft cows and make cheese. They do all kinds of things. Right now they're very interested in asparagus.

". . . As of now we have twenty-five hectares, not much, right? But we spend our whole life on them, and on top of that there are the chickens and pigs. But being enthusiastic is the least of it, of course, here the point is what you do."

"In what sense?"

But the meal was over and Ilya stood up.

"I'll get back to the sense another time, forgive me." He smiled. "I have to go. I didn't purposely lead you to the sense, that was accidental. And it may not interest you. Vasya here, for instance, finds it totally inimical."

"You think Vasya and I have something in common?"

"Yes," Ilya said after a moment's thought, "but his life is even harder than yours. He's never had a foothold."

Shaibin stood up too.

"It's like you've dug your heels into the prewar era," Ilya went on, "and you're reaching for it with all your might, but he has no foothold, just the feeble era of war and revolution. And you, with all you have to lean on—that foothold brings you joy, right? You wouldn't mind perishing, isn't that so? Basically, you want to share Russia's fate, even though Russia's fate, and consequently your future, is very dim. Well, but Vasya has no foothold and no Russia, and therein lies the irremediable horror. He's searching for roots and has no wish to perish."

"But where is the similarity?" Shaibin asked, as if he wanted to catch Ilya out.

"The similarity is tremendous. You and he have the same inner face. You both don't know where happiness lies."

When Ilya spoke these words he was already in the doorway, but Shaibin managed to catch up with him.

"And you, do you know where happiness lies?" he asked in a muffled voice, grabbing Ilya's sleeve.

Ilya glanced quickly at that large, slender hand.

"Yes," he said, "but you're too proud for it." And blushing suddenly, he ran down the front steps, shuffling his canvas shoes straight through the manure spread out there yesterday, and was gone.

Shaibin went down into the orchard, where he felt entirely out of place. The vegetable garden was empty, patches of earth were covered in manure; next to that, evidently, they were transplanting cabbage, lettuce, onions, and leeks. In this poor season of late September, all there was poking up in the beds were the remnants of the former glory of eggplants, cucumbers, red cabbage, Brussels sprouts, and cauliflower (but a special, autumn variety). On the other hand, the trees dangled their fruits all over the orchard: pears, apples, plums, and peaches glowed on sturdy branches, golden, pink, dull purple, fragrant. Shaibin went down, not toward the road, but in the opposite direction, where he thought Ilya had gone. Here there were two stone outbuildings, and a huge ox face was looking out the doorway of one of them, dumb and wise at the same time. Chickens were cackling in the henhouse. A shaggy dog was shuffling its feet here, barely glancing at Shaibin. He walked past it, skirted a rickety fence, where a chick that had strayed that morning fell underfoot, and came out on the path to the field.

How many years since he'd been in fields? He tried not to think about that. His head spun when he looked at the birds flying toward him. When he reached a solitary branching maple that had grown up by the boundary strip, he abruptly stretched out beneath it on the warm autumn earth. In front of him was the very area that Ilya had set aside for wheat, surprising the entire district.

October, the month of major sowing, had not yet begun, and in anticipation of the winter crops the earth lay under an even swath of potash and sulfate. The air was blue and clear. Shaibin stretched out prone. He saw trembling blades of grass and an impetuous ant . . . All of a sudden he threw his arms out and touched cheek and forehead to this hard, scratchy earth. And then the strange spasm he was so ashamed of, the legacy of a campaign lost long ago, cramped his face.

When he came to, he heard Marianna singing a Provençal song so long that no one knew how it ended. The song told of a simple peasant girl; a rich stranger falls in love with her; and she conceives a child by him and goes to town, where she betrays him with a poor thatcher from her village.

CHAPTER THREE

IT WAS FULL dark when Vera Kirillovna threw a Russian shawl over her shoulders, carefully shut the house's creaky door, and walked past the last rows of pear trees, where in the summer they had raised flowers and where now, in the dry coolness of the autumn night, there was a long, unflinching silence.

Were they really meeting? She didn't have long to wait. Ilya locked the cowshed, slipped the key in his pocket, and went down through the orchard to join her. The night was starry beyond the forest, the same forest where the surveyors had been working that afternoon, and a smooth, gelatinous moon was just about to emerge.

"Ilyusha," Vera Kirillovna called out.

They went as far as the gate in silence and came out on the road.

"Ilyusha, what is this? Is Vasya leaving?" Vera Kirillovna asked in despair. "I read the letter. Gorbatov has sent Kellerman for him. All those years it wasn't that he couldn't adapt or find his place, the way you and I thought, no, he spent two months in prison in Chelyabinsk, where they found him in 1920, and then, it turns out, he immediately took an important post in Siberia and now he's head of the fur trust. Are you listening?"

"Yes, Mama."

"Now he's living in Moscow and has Kellerman under him, and evidently Kellerman's here on business. Adolf hasn't been luring Vasya a whole year for nothing. He's in on it. You can tell from the letter that Stepan needs one of you, and he's simply demanding Kellerman make that happen. Even if Vasya doesn't care—it's an absolutely straightforward transaction. The problem is that external circumstances have coincided here with Vasya's own impulse. Am I right?"

"Yes," Ilya replied. "Vasya's wish has coincided with external circumstances. His wish is very strong, ferocious even, a blind wish that's suddenly found a way to come true. It's not adventure or freedom luring him. If it were, he'd just latch on to someone and go to Paris or Africa. He's looking to find a foothold—he doesn't feel it inside himself—and right now for him that foothold is Gorbatov and Gorbatov's Russia."

Vera Kirillovna wrapped her shawl around her. The edge of a red moon had come into view.

"But Vasya is one of those people," Ilya went on, "who invest too much meaning in external conditions. If there were no visa, ticket, and money, do you really think he'd have the passion to leave here? Never. If Adolf's letters were to stop, if this connection with Gorbatov were broken, he would stay. This rebellion against our life, against you and me, is at base a rebellion for the idleness he thinks he'll get there. He calls it roots, but I think it's having an easy life. Actually, maybe roots are a part of an easy life. You and I have always sought out the hardest life . . . But left to Vasya's emotional forces alone, this rebellion would stop by itself. Not because the rebellion isn't strong enough or deep enough—no, for Vasya it's very deep, I can see he has God knows what going on inside of him now—but because Vasya is the kind of person who gets carried off and away by life's conditions."

"Maybe if the old man who came this morning—"

"Did you see him? Talk to him?"

"Yes. It seems to me he may not survive the winter, and the girl will end up with us. She looks older than she is and she has no one . . ."

"But I wanted to finish up about Vasya. Tomorrow I'm going to Paris and I'll see Kellerman. If he backs off, Vasya won't leave. Vasya will wait for me to return. There's nothing else to be done."

They turned around and went back toward the house.

"Make him swear," Vera Kirillovna said, "otherwise he'll leave. Every night I'm afraid he's going to leave."

They walked a few moments in silence.

"Should I expect just you from Paris?" Vera Kirillovna asked, her question flashing her dark, affectionate gaze straight into his eyes.

"Oh, Mama," Ilya exclaimed, embarrassed, taking her arm, "there's not another soul like yours in the whole world."

"And there's not another like you either," she said firmly. "So will it be just you?"

"Just me," Ilya replied. "It can't be otherwise."

The vegetable plot shone in front of them, white in the moonlight, the shadows lying perfectly still and distinct.

It was probably about ten o'clock. The house had that slightly uncertain look that can happen when there are people sleeping inside. Ilya climbed the steep shuddering stairs to the attic; up top, black in the moonlight, he called down to Vera Kirillovna one last time.

"Mama, two words, the last thing I need to tell you. On Sunday, Jolifleur is coming to ask for Marianna's hand. Ask them exactly when the money is going to be sent for the Parisian party, and I'll alert them once and for all. They're waiting."

Vera Kirillovna nodded silently and went inside. She knew how to move unusually quietly. In the dim light she saw that Marianna had taken the bed into the kitchen and Shaibin was sleeping on it, covered in his waterproof coat. The window wasn't fully shut. She stood there and listened. His nose, fine and sharp, was white in the weak moonlight and his numb arm hung to the floor.

A shudder passed through Vera Kirillovna; she dared not move. The thought that Marianna was nearby brought her around. Yes, Marianna was lying selflessly on the floor, having spread a blanket underneath herself and thrown an old, scorched scarf over her legs. Her hair was a tangled shock, her fresh shoulders and small maidenly chest were uncovered, and her arms, her large, valiant arms, were flung wide so that Vera Kirillovna had to step over one of them. This was how Gabriel would soon be seeing her.

But Vasya wasn't asleep. He was sitting without a candle. The attic was low and empty; the window here was left open winter and summer. Two old field cots stood to either side of it, and Vasya was sitting on his in just his shirt. He could see the stars but only guess at the moon.

He was sleepy, and twice already he'd lost his sense of reality. He'd begun to dream the same dream: under Marianna's pillow, under the one where Shaibin now slept, he knows there's an envelope. "Swear you won't touch it!" Ilya says, but he reaches in, and the paper, stiff, on the thin pillow, crackles in his hand. And then someone's cool, slender fingers try to take the letter away from him; their touch is agonizing and sweet, and he drops the envelope, he wants to catch that hand, but it disappears and he doesn't even know whose it was. It feels painful and bizarre.

Both times he woke up. Why? Because of the silence, the rustling of dog paws outside the window, and the light nighttime chill sensible to his naked knees and bared thigh. When Ilya came in and the door sang a long fifth, Vasya got up and immediately felt the night chill, to the point of shivering, and knowing he wouldn't fall asleep for anything now he slipped under his blanket.

Ilya walked past the empty vats and the old workbench under the acrid-smelling horse harness that hung there—an extra not once taken off its hook in all this time. It was dark in the corners, and you could have touched the stars. Ilya sat down on Vasya's bed.

"Move your legs."

Vasya stirred obediently.

"Was there a check in the letter?" Ilya asked.

"Yes."

"For how much?"

"Three thousand."

Ilya took off his canvas shoes, propped his bare feet on his own bed, and started rolling tobacco.

"They're buying you, Vasily," he said, shaking his head. "You unhappy child!"

Vasya slid all the way under the blanket. He replied in a stifled voice.

"I'll leave you the money, Ilya. I'm causing you losses by quitting my job. According to our terms you can ask me to pay you back."

"Have you lost your mind? We didn't have terms, you were always free. I had my way three years ago plotting all this. You didn't have to agree. But you were sixteen. Now you're free to do whatever you like."

"There's another question here." Vasya was clearly agonizing. "You're not obligated to support Mama. She won't take anything from Father, but from me . . ."

"Quit playing the fool. You only think you have to talk like this in your position."

They sat in silence for a few minutes. Smoke went straight from Ilya into the deep blue of the window, where it dissipated.

"You've been unlucky with us, Ilya," Vasya said suddenly, almost defiantly. "Both Marianna and I want to live the opposite way to you."

"Leave Marianna out of it."

"Isn't that so? Weren't you against mixed marriage? Or have you yielded that position?"

"Leave Marianna out of it," he repeated. "It's all right for us, on the land."

Ilya collected the right words in his thoughts, and Monsieur Jolifleur's ruddy face and then the wayfarer's voice raced through his memory. Their all too brief encounter was an unconscious weight on Ilya's heart.

Vasya propped himself up on his elbow.

"Why?" he asked, agitated.

"Because the land . . . *C'est tout autre chose.* Anyway, let's not talk about that for now."

Vasya's head dropped back on the pillow.

"For now . . . No, you just don't have an answer for me," he said with a grin. "Your plans are collapsing one after the other and your convictions are proving useless. I'm going one way, Marianna another. Life is proving you wrong."

"And I repeat that I'll never agree to your theory of two solutions. I'll spend my whole life proving there's a third."

"You're saving yourself?"

"You ask that with an irony you can't answer—you're ashamed of yourself. This is my life, and there's your whole answer. I chose it myself, it didn't just happen . . . But I don't want to talk about myself anymore or argue with you. Tomorrow I'm going to Paris."

"I understood that from today's conversations."

"And I want your consent. You're surprised? As you realize, I'm going to see Kellerman. Wait for me, tell me you won't set out until I return."

"Fine, but why?"

"You give me your word?"

"Yes. I want to say goodbye to you. When will you be back?"

"Tomorrow's Friday. I'll start back Monday evening."

"Which means I'll set out on Tuesday."

"Is that your decision no matter what? It's irrevocable?"

"Which means I'll set out on Tuesday," Vasya repeated stubbornly.

Ilya lowered his feet and pushed himself back to the edge of Vasya's bed.

"What if I get Kellerman to release you?"

"It's too late. First of all, they think you're some kind of Tolstoyan . . ."

Ilya shuddered.

"Secondly, it's too late. I can't anymore. Living here means perishing."

"You can't? Do you really think you'll be able to there?"

"I'll have roots there." Vasya spoke softly.

"In the Gorbatov trust, you mean?"

They fell silent again. Ilya spoke up.

"No, Vasya, you want happiness no matter what, but you don't know where it lies . . . You want idleness, change, some kind of antediluvian emotional depravity. You really are an awful lot like Shaibin."

"And what's Shaibin?"

"As Mama says, 'a formerly marvelous person.' I think there are an awful lot of those formerly marvelous people, especially in Paris. And what are they for?"

"Oh, you're becoming hard, Ilyusha."

"Being hard isn't such a bad thing, especially when it helps someone not to forgive someone something."

"Does it help you?"

"Yes. I can't and don't want to forgive."

"Who? Our father?"

"Our father above all. And then one other person."

"I know who."

66

"You do? All right. Fine. I don't think I'd have it in me to say his name."

"It's Shaibin!" Vasya said distinctly.

Ilya turned slightly, but Vasya, curled up under the blanket, could still see his face.

"The best woman in the world loved him!" Ilya said with difficulty.

"The best in the world," Vasya echoed.

"He's more intense than you by nature, you know?" Ilya went on. "He's better than you, Vasya. All his life he's had a fire in him that you don't have."

"Why are you comparing me to him?"

"Because you have the same diabolical unrest in you. But he does his ruining and perishing consciously and passionately, while you . . . my poor Vasya!"

Those last few words tore from Ilya's lips almost inadvertently; it wasn't him, it was his very soul saying that. At the same time he felt Vasya's breath on his face.

"And you think I don't feel sorry for myself, Ilyusha?" he whispered, and that whisper held something of the child that all too recently had gone missing in him, suddenly and crudely, for good, it seemed. "My God, how sorry I feel for myself!"

Ilya saw his light eyes so near to his. They were full of tears.

"Stay," he said quietly but distinctly, taking Vasya's hand.

Vasya looked away; his hand remained in Ilya's rough hands.

"No," he said, fighting tears. "I can't. Go to Paris and come back quickly. I want to see Gorbatov, I want to look at him all caught up there, and I want to get all caught up alongside him."

Ilya lightly tugged at his shirtsleeve.

"Stay," he said again, "for Mama's sake." And he gave him a quick kiss. Vasya shuddered.

"She forgives me," he said, his teeth chattering, "she forgives me for the 'Gorbatov poison,' as she puts it."

Ilya stood up and walked to the window. He began undressing. Vasya pulled the blanket up over his head.

"Would you like to split off with the pigs?" Ilya asked suddenly. "I'll arrange everything for you and you can start living freely."

Vasya didn't stir.

"I don't need it, I don't need your love." Ilya could barely make out his voice. "Forgive me."

He lay there perfectly still for a long time. Ilya undressed and lay down. Sleep snuck up on him. Suddenly Vasya sat up in bed.

"And you're going to come back from Paris and shovel manure?" he asked ringingly.

"Yes."

"And sow wheat?"

"Yes."

He shook his head to the right and left and balled up his fists.

"No, I can't," he said with a flash of anger. "I was five when war was declared. I hate everyone."

He buried his head in his pillow so he couldn't see the sky, or the window, or Ilya.

And almost immediately both fell into a heavy sleep.

In the morning, Shaibin told Vera Kirillovna and Marianna that he was going to Paris with Ilya. No one saw Ilya until evening. He showed up for an early supper already dressed for town.

His cap and half-empty suitcase appeared with him. Marianna put two bottles of red Vaucluse on the table. Vasya drank more than anyone. As was his habit, he sat sideways to the table, but this did not disturb the rather solemn, brief, almost mute meal. It was not yet seven when Ilya and Shaibin started on their journey. It was three kilometers to town, the same town where Monsieur Jolifleur had his Au Paradis-Chevalin. A railroad branch led from there straight to

A., where it intersected with the main Paris–Lyons–Mediterranean line.

The travelers were supposed to catch the nine-thirty express.

The sun was setting and birds were swarming over the fields. Vera Kirillovna, however, did not go down to the gate; Shaibin leaned toward her on the porch and asked her something.

"I'll tell you if you write," she said calmly. He took ten steps and suddenly turned around and ran back toward the house. Possibly he'd forgotten his African pipe on the table. He remained in the house for a couple of minutes, no more. When he came out, his face was wet. Shaibin had been crying? Oh, no! Those were Vera Kirillovna's tears.

Vasya walked them both as far as the main road. A rickety bus happened to be passing. Ilya flagged it down and the wheels screeched to a halt; both got in. An old woman was holding two roosters at her low-hanging, withered breasts, three men in dickeys were returning to town from a wedding, each with a boutonniere in his lapel. The bus likely had had some connection to the wedding; streamers were heaped on the shaking floor.

When Ilya and Shaibin boarded the train it was nearly dark, and by the time they transferred in

A.—under lights, in the train-station smoke—night had fallen.

They ended up alone in a narrow, smoke-filled third-class section. From here and all the way to Lyons the train would race at furious speed, and outside, occasionally, in the night's black gloom, what looked like a dead arm would flash and the lights of villages and towns would swim vaguely behind it. Meanwhile, in the train car, Arabs sang and sailors shouted, shooting craps; children cried, the night train creaked.

Shaibin sat in the corner and immediately felt that train physicality he had loved since childhood: while the wheels are racing you feel like jumping up, a deceptive alarm wrenches your heart, and you get the urge to leap and hit the ground chest first. But no sooner does it fall still at a station than a massive indolence lashes at your legs and entwines all of you, and you can't move, even to drink some beer, even to find out what the newsboy holding the big-city newspaper is shouting about there.

He sat down in the corner across from Ilya; Ilya was his for the whole night. Hadn't he dreamed of this encounter during those African nights? He was going to Paris to see Nyusha Slyotova and had stayed with the Gorbatovs to see Vera Kirillovna. But hadn't the hidden purpose of it all been Ilya himself? Now, as he began to think, what was revealed was a kind of delirium.

Yesterday, he had still found Ilya a mystery, connected to Nyusha, and only that. He'd seen in Ilya a rival, someone she loved who'd taken his place in her heart. Now Ilya had become more than a rival for him, he was an enemy, but what an enemy! Shaibin had never had enemies like this before.

This person held the keys to what Shaibin had been searching for his whole life. But those keys were the kind you couldn't steal; in Shaibin's hands they would lose all their valuable properties. Ilya himself would have to open the longed-for doors for Shaibin, and Ilya himself guide him somewhere by his own hand. But for that he had to be converted from enemy to friend— maybe more than a friend, maybe a brother . . .

He looked at Ilya the way he had at the table and once again wished he could open him up and look inside and read all the answers. He felt the Nyusha riddle becoming just one part of that enormous riddle Ilya posed by his entire existence. Yes, for Alexei Ivanovich Shaibin, despite all his vehemence, the thought of Nyusha was sometimes vanquished effort-lessly by the thought of Ilya.

He wanted to open Ilya up and look inside him, but his silly, fainthearted fear that Ilya himself would inadvertently reveal the crucial thing that would suddenly change Shaibin's whole life had vanished. "Hold out hope"—no, he no longer had that humiliating desire. Now he actually felt the thirst for battle that was so rare for him and that was always harnessed to suffering.

But this made it even harder for the conversation to begin.

"Are you going to sleep?" Ilya asked, smoking in silence the whole time.

"No, I'd rather listen to you if you would tell me something," Shaibin replied and he turned up his coat collar.

Ilya couldn't help but smile at him, and Shaibin wished he could find irony or superiority in that smile. But it held neither one nor the other.

"Would you like to hear it all, the way it was?" Ilya said simply. "If that's what you want, Alexei Ivanovich, but you'll be disappointed. You probably know it all from her letters already, and there wasn't even very much of it!"

Shaibin felt an inward shudder, perhaps because here, right now, just past Montélimar, the weather had changed abruptly. All of a sudden, the man who had lived in Africa for three years found the forgotten north suspect. He stood up, shut the door to the corridor, which was letting in the pernicious freshness, and sat back down, shoving his hands into his pockets.

"I got to know her in Paris," Ilya went on. "I saw her five or six times. Then I left, and then Mama and the children joined me. A month later, more or less, she wrote to me. We've continued to correspond ever since. And that's it."

Ilya fell silent. The train car was rocking from side to side.

"And that's it? Well, I know much more." Shaibin grinned. "You are by no means the simpleton you make yourself out to be, Ilya. You know how to maintain a very clever silence."

Ilya looked him keenly in the eyes.

"Oh, no, Alexei Ivanovich, I'm no simpleton, and I'm warning you of this before it's too late. Just because I settled on the land doesn't mean I turned into a sweet, naïve simpleton. For God's sake don't make that mistake."

"And you're not going to tell me anything more?" Shaibin asked more calmly.

"No, Alexei Ivanovich, I have nothing more to tell you. But I know very little of you too, starting with the fact that Nyusha never once mentioned your name, if nothing else. Only now do I realize it was you."

"What did she write you about me?"

"That she didn't know you long, that you loved both her and her sister, that after you left, her sister took poison, and that then Nyusha would have followed you to the ends of the earth. But now . . ."

"Go on!"

"But now—she wouldn't."

In the dim car Shaibin turned white.

"I'm cold," he said. "This isn't Africa."

The Arab had reminded him of Africa. He was standing in the corridor by the window and was visible through the glass in the door. The wind was fluttering his white clothing, which from a distance looked angelically pure. He was eating plums and spitting the slippery pits into the black forest rushing toward them. An enormous angel was eating plums in the night; he, like Shaibin, was afraid of the north.

"And Marianna?" Shaibin asked suddenly. "She's getting married?"

Ilya nodded.

"Yes. I can tell you about Marianna too. She's marrying Gabriel Jolifleur, the son of the man who owns Au Paradis-Chevalin."

"Do you see some meaning in that too?"

"I do now. Before, I used to fear this, I fought this. Assimilation is a terrible wrong, second to returnism, but in this case—I find this hard to explain, I'm still letting this settle—in this case it may even be a good. And you know who convinced me of this? Jolifleur himself and one other person. Jolifleur understood me immediately. He said that at first he'd been wary, as I was, but now he knew that this was right. Oh, if you knew what an unusual man he is! All day among horse carcasses, the blood dripping, but you come on Sunday and he talks about what's most vital. My old boss is his friend. My old boss is the mayor of Saint-Didier, and Jolifleur is on the council too, and both believe in certain opportunities. But that's a secret."

"What kind of secret?"

"I can't, it's not mine. It concerns the free farms on the far side of Saint-Didier and expanding the canning factory. Truth be told—the whole business is in asparagus."

"Asparagus?" Shaibin exclaimed, struck, and all of a sudden he felt like bursting into laughter.

"Yes, but I've spilled too much as it is."

"You've spilled? That's your good fortune, Ilya, and my ill fortune is that you could never spill anything. But wait a minute. Tell me more. Is your own brother fleeing to Russia because of this asparagus?"

"He's going to Russia, and you to Paris," Ilya said drily. "I told him you two were alike. He just came too late. He couldn't be like you, since he's of our generation. Why should he be doomed to suffer the way you do?"

Shaibin shrugged.

"And nonetheless you think you can prevent him from going? You're on your way to Paris now, which means you have hope?"

"I have no hope, Alexei Ivanovich. I have to do everything I'm doing."

"Is that the only reason you're going?"

"No, not the only one." Ilya blushed. "I'm going to see Nyusha, but that's not all of it either."

A woman passed down the corridor, swaying from the movement of the car, and her queasy, dark-lipped face glanced at them in their compartment. They were silent for a long time—long enough for the woman to come back the other way.

"You mean Vasya's a 'last,' too?" Shaibin suddenly asked, leaning toward Ilya.

"On your lips 'last' is like a watchword, Alexei Ivanovich."

"Answer me."

"Yes, a 'last.'"

"And you still want to do everything for him? But wait a minute. Maybe you're prepared to do everything for me too? Maybe even yesterday you'd decided all this and this journey is no coincidence? And these conversations are your tactic?"

"I have no hopes, Alexei Ivanovich. This time has taught me to act without hope. Before, people probably thought that was impossible and action itself had to suffer as a result. Now everything's changed. Yes, even for you . . . I have to do everything. But you know I'm not alone in this—as I'm not, actually, in the matter with Vasya."

Ilya recalled standing under the moon with Vera Kirillovna the previous night and twice kissing the silky part in her hair.

He couldn't see Alexei Ivanovich's face now. Several minutes passed.

"Ilya, you truly are an unusually fine person, as Nyusha calls you," Shaibin said at last, agitated. "And I don't know whether to thank you or reproach you for all the things you didn't tell me today."

He stood up and wrapped his coat around him. The thought of the forgotten northern dawn that was going to stir in the window in a few hours pierced him with melancholy. He walked to the door. How the wheels rumbled! How long the night rails clanked!

"Alexei Ivanovich, what is Africa like?" Ilya asked suddenly.

"It's a place anyone can go to at any time."

"You don't want to tell me about your life?"

"No."

"You were in the Foreign Legion?"

"Yes."

"How did you get out of there?"

"They discharged me due to illness . . ."

"What illness do you have?"

"Heart."

"You were unwell?"

"I already said I don't want to tell you."

"Then answer me this. Is there any possibility of sending for men there who are finishing up their enlistment? To work?"

Shaibin swiftly looked around.

"What are you asking? You're a maniac!"

He returned to his seat. He wanted to fully understand what they had actually been talking about this whole time. What had he learned that apparently had changed him? Nyusha? Yes, Nyusha, and something else too.

"So you think I can be saved?" he asked into space.

Ilya wasn't accustomed to conversations like this, and Shaibin was exhausting him.

"You guessed that long ago," he said harshly. "Why do you ask?"

"And what will you do about Nyusha?" Shaibin asked, sensing he was beyond stopping himself.

But Ilya neither knew how nor wanted to give in. He watched Shaibin's inward trembling gradually emerge on the outside: his teeth started chattering. And suddenly the coming day appeared before Ilya like a whirlwind of sinister events akin to this night-time rumble of train cars and the engine's roar. He saw the dim streets he would have to roam, the buildings inhabited by people who weren't his own but weren't strangers either, and so clearly did his heart feel the approach of this difficult life that for one instant he was close to grabbing Shaibin by the arm and compulsively revealing what he couldn't reveal and asking him the impossible.

CHAPTER FOUR

S HAIBIN OPENED THE tap and boiling hot water gushed into the basin. Steam rose in the small, dusty room and clouded the mirror and window, obscuring everything for minutes. Shaibin opened the other tap, the cold one, and waited for the water to warm up, washed his face, hands, and neck, and dried off with a rough towel. He was in a hurry, he had to be on time no matter what.

He barely ran a wet brush through his long, thinning hair. How he hated all these essential movements! He changed his collar and wiped off his terrible boots with what came to hand. He had very little time.

But Ilya didn't come out. His door, next to Shaibin's, was closed, and it was quiet inside. Shaibin went up a floor. No one followed him. Here the hallway was a little darker and a gas jet was burning at the far end. Shaibin nearly tripped over a pile of dirty sheets taken from an open room. He went to the end of the hallway twice in search of the right door. His former wanderings were ending and new ones beginning at this door.

He knocked, but no one answered. He knocked again, trying not to think how he would go in, what he would say—he'd thought about this too much. She's not alone! the repulsive thought flashed in him.

"Who's there?" a woman's voice asked.

And Shaibin walked in, pulled the door shut, and turned the key behind him.

Much later he would remember this moment and be unable to recall anything but his happiness and horror. And also: the edge of a red silk skirt poking out of a half-shut mirrored armoire.

Nyusha lay under a fluffy comforter; the room was dim, and she didn't turn her head toward the door right away.

"Shaibin?" she said when she had taken a close look at the visitor. "But what time is it?"

He didn't say anything. The room was hot and smelled of perfume and cigarettes, and Nyusha's things were tossed all about: her underwear, her stockings, her purse, even her hat, even her fur coat.

"I'm asking you, what time is it? Have you gone deaf, Alyosha?" Only then did Shaibin notice the clock on her nightstand.

She flung back the comforter but still lay there, and only then did he see her: she had cut her hair short, she had lost weight, she was completely different.

"I see you're upset," she said, raising a brow. "Hang my coat on the nail and hand me my purse. There's a chair for you."

He handed her the purse. She put on lipstick, lit a cigarette, and sat up a little. Her hair was blond and curled behind her ears, and her ears themselves—small and even—were just like tea roses: light at the edges and deep pink in the middle.

"Here for long, Alyosha?" she asked, taking her time examining him since he had not sat down. "Straight from Marseilles?"

"No, I stopped off to see the Gorbatovs."

"The Gorbatovs? And?"

"And nothing. Marianna is getting married."

"To a marquis?"

"No, a butcher."

"What about Ilya?" she asked ingenuously.

"Ilya's here."

"Here!" she cried out, sitting up on the bed and dropping her cigarette on the rug. "Since when?"

Shaibin didn't answer.

"I was joking," he said, blanching. "He's planning to and told me to send his regards . . . Next week maybe . . ."

"How you've aged!" she said coldly. "And from your letters I thought you were still the same."

The room was so cramped that, sitting in the chair, Shaibin could touch the table with one hand and the bed with the other. What did the window look out on? There, outside, it was so quiet and dark that it was starting to bother him. But Nyusha's things were here, by his side, the things that meant too much to him, that had such power over him and humiliated him in a way no single living being had ever humiliated him.

Here were her gloves, expensive, rabbit skin, with a design at the wrist, small and probably always warm and a little alive; here were her curved scissors without which she could not last a day and which were constantly getting lost; here lay her colorful, window-pane-check silk scarf and her yellow-bound book, and someone's note; hanging from the chair, her pale stockings fell straight into the shoes placed beneath, and he wanted to weep over the pile of ribbons, the garters and silk, wanted to breathe in that silk, his head buried in it.

"How early you've come," Nyusha said. "I was still asleep."

He dropped his head for a moment.

"Give me your hand," he said. "You still haven't greeted me."

She held out her gentle, warm hand with the short pink nails.

"Do you know why I've come?" he asked, kissing her palm. "I've come to marry you."

She pulled her hand back and closed her eyes.

"Alyosha," she said, "I know you too well. I'm bored with you. If I say no, you'll turn pale and start kissing my feet. If I say yes, you . . . you might not marry me anyway."

"Quiet, quiet!"

"But I'm saying no anyway. Not because I can't forgive you Lyuba's death. After all, she left a little girl. Just think, in our day and age! And not because you abandoned me three years ago. I'm saying no because I simply can't anymore with people like you. I'm too much like you myself. Leave me in peace."

Shaibin moved over to her bed. She shifted away from him and pulled up the blanket.

"There has to be an end to any and all anxiety," she said. "Don't embrace me."

"You find me repulsive?"

"You're misunderstanding me. I don't find you repulsive. You're brother to my soul, but I find being with you awkward and difficult. I can't anymore."

"Do you love someone else?"

"Yes."

She turned away sullenly, and her eyelashes scratched the pillow.

"Ilya?"

Shaibin leaned toward her face. Once again she recognized those lips, that strong round chin, those eyes.

"Ilya," she said.

At that moment he touched her lips. She struggled in his arms, but her own arms were under the blanket and he held her down. He roughly spread her cool lips and she fell still.

The time could only be guessed at in that room; the window faced a wall. Which was why it was so quiet. The street was far away. Shaibin released Nyusha and sat back down; his hands were shaking.

"You're not curious about me," he said, "and there's no love without curiosity."

Nyusha didn't move.

"There's tenderness," she said quietly, "the same kind I have for myself. But don't force your kiss on me again, Alyosha. How can you force a kiss on me after the way we once made love?"

And she looked at him as if she wanted to resurrect precious and terrible moments in her memory.

"Let me see you," he said in a muffled voice.

She shook her head.

"Alyosha, there won't be any of that. I have enough anxiety of my own. We can't be together. We would both be lost."

"You mean you want to save yourself?" he asked coarsely.

She looked at him sadly for a minute.

"I do."

"You shouldn't be saving yourself, you should be letting someone support you," he said.

This didn't fluster her. She made a movement with her head, and her hair fell over her eyes. Then she didn't move for a long time. One might have thought she wasn't breathing, so still was her body under the rough blue blanket.

What was Alexei Ivanovich standing here for now? It was time for him to go. Where? Back to the station, to catch that same train to that same South. But weren't human actions like this basically ridiculous? Shaibin picked up one of her gloves and pressed it to his face. Was this really the sole thing left him?

"Nyusha," he called to her.

She slowly turned her head toward him.

"No, Alyosha," she said a little proudly. "You can be a 'last' if you want, but I don't. Maybe I'll latch on to something and won't perish. But our old life is over."

"You don't need me?" he asked in agony.

She shook her head.

"An answer is what I need," he said quietly, "but you're just as much in the dark as I am."

Then a wild sadness gripped Shaibin. He stood up, threw the glove on the table, and took a step toward the bed.

"Your answer is downstairs," he said furiously. "Room thirty-four. He deigned to arrive with me today and, as you see, he still hasn't come to see you."

His last words jumbled together in his mouth. He turned, banged his knee on the table, unlocked the door, and went out. Nyusha ran after him in just her nightshirt and stuck her head into the hallway.

"Alyosha!" she exclaimed. Shaibin didn't look around. He went down all three flights, his heart beating desperately. Up until now he hadn't taken note of the city or the streets. He descended the stairs to them the way a drunk descends to the bottom of his own drunken slough.

The day was as promised. An early fog hung between the buildings. The asphalt gleamed. Although it hadn't rained, everything was damp: the boulevard's benches, the streetlamps, the cold stone. Shaibin walked past a few shops, crossed the wide street overhung with the drone of automobile horns, and set off through unfamiliar side streets in the direction he imagined the cemetery should be.

There, above the mortuary crypts, there was a bridge crossed by lumbering buses and ringing, rumbling streetcars. The aerial street bisected the cemetery. To this day, those streets hacked through on different planes of the city seemed somehow monstrous to Shaibin. In Paris, he'd known them in the most idyllic neighborhoods, but to this day the London he had once seen somewhere not far from Tower Bridge and the black two-story streets of Whitechapel was a soul-crushing nightmare of a memory.

The poisoned greenery under the bridge didn't stir, and the overfull crypts were deaf. Shaibin walked back, down the sloping pavement, to the wall. Hearses were parked by the gate, and the hairy torchbearers perched on them, drunk from the white Bordeaux they'd been drinking on an empty stomach since early morning, were talking about nothing in particular.

Shaibin went down the first path he came to. It smelled of the rot of municipal gardens, where the earth had long been saturated with cigarette butts nine centimeters deep and in the summer birds silently choked. A little girl wearing round eyeglasses and a short burnous was walking down the path. Shaibin stopped and watched her go. He was searching inside himself for injured pride—no, that he didn't have. His absence of pride, like his divided self, also bore the stamp of time.

Everything, everything bore the stamp of time, even the fact that he'd ended up at the cemetery now. And it was a good time, a blessed time, at least that's what Ilya said. But he, Alexei Shaibin, he was choking on it. Once upon a time Nyusha, too, had choked on it in joyous despair, but she didn't want to choke anymore, she was searching for burning new rays of light. Someone had already doused her with a faint wave of invisible oxygen.

She turned back from the door, lit the light in the room, and, both fearing and not believing, began to dress. A silk stocking, the same one Shaibin had just been prepared to weep over, tore and ran. Nyusha rifled through the armoire and found another. She put on a short woolen dress, combed her hair off her round forehead and behind her ears—there, under the comb, it curled thickly—Nyusha had started wearing her hair this way only recently—and then she found her low-heeled brown shoes and fastened them with a hook. No, truly, Ilya hadn't come!

The chaos of this room, in artificial light at eleven o'clock in the morning, was unbearable. Nyusha moved jerkily. She was tall and skinny, her legs were too thin, and her shoulders perhaps too fragile. She checked the mirror a couple of times. There was something inexplicably simple, modest, and clear about her, despite her puffy red mouth and long mascaraed lashes. Or had she rushed to get dressed to no end? Unconsciously dawdling, she reread the note that had been lying on her table since the previous evening:

> I was there at nine-thirty, as arranged. I think there has to be an end to all the lying. If you couldn't be home yesterday, you shouldn't play games with me.—*A.K.*

Ilya still hadn't come.

Suddenly she started dashing around the room, threw her coat over her shoulders, turned off the light, and opened the curtains—and the hopeless day peeked in. She walked to the door, went back, took her handkerchief off the nightstand, and wadded it up. With a distracted glance at her unmade bed, finally, she went out. No, no one was on the stairs.

A shred of doubt remained in her heart as she descended. The smell of her perfume lingered after her in the dark hallway. She crossed the deserted landing openly; she knew that at this hour she wouldn't see anyone who lived there: Berta, Natasha, and Merichka were all still asleep. But the maid heard her steps. She came out of the room Shaibin had occupied, and seeing someone knocking at the next door said, "Monsieur is not in."

The room was too quiet—or so it seemed to Nyusha.

"He left?" she asked, and her coat slipped off her shoulder.

"Monsieur is not in," the maid repeated. "He didn't even open his suitcase."

They looked at each other for another half minute. Then the maid straightened the scarf on her head, and her broom began whistling over the frieze carpet.

The key was dangling in the lock; forgetting herself, Nyusha turned it and walked in. Ilya hadn't touched a thing. Just one of the towels was crumpled and lay on the floor, and his suitcase was tossed on the bed. Without closing the door, Nyusha took two steps toward the suitcase; it wasn't locked. She opened it. On top lay Marianna's note: "Ilyusha! Bring me a present of lilac soap, the kind they wash with in Paris." Nyusha let the lid drop. It occurred to her that she could wait for Ilya here, sitting on the table, her feet resting on the armchair. But she was afraid he wouldn't be back until evening. Truth be told, she didn't quite understand her fear herself; she simply felt a strong, secret longing.

And then, still holding her coat close, she left the room and went downstairs to the telephone. Just like yesterday, people were moving around, and it smelled of cooking. Nyusha went over to the telephone and picked up the receiver. She had business that simply could not be put off any longer, she had to respond to Adolf Kellerman's note from yesterday.

The building where Alexander Adolfovich Kellerman rented a furnished apartment for himself, his wife, and his son was enormous and located on a broad, quiet street between the Champs-Élysées and a quay of the Seine. Half the windows were tightly shuttered; most of its inhabitants weren't expected to return to the city for another week, not before, either from Biarritz, or from the waters of the great and pure Lake Annecy, or from remote and luxurious Auvergne. The marble staircase Ilya ascended, not without revulsion, was carpeted, and there were tropical plants placed here and there by the mirrors. A year ago, at his father's behest, Adolf had come here with his mother to study shipbuilding and sports, a precipitous journey from their packed apartment on Nastasinsky Lane, where there was the imminent threat of his departure for military service.

In his not too distant but now thoroughly forgotten childhood years, Adolf had attended the same Soviet school as Vasya and Marianna. At the time, old Kellerman was not yet a connoisseur of the fur trade such as Gorbatov would make of him during the years of the New Economic Policy, when Gorbatov himself (at what price?) had turned up at the head of one of the Siberian trusts, and not in the capacity of a has-been, as you'd expect, monitoring expenditures, which required an unswerving eye, but in the capacity of the eye itself ... Under Gorbatov, Kellerman, too, revived, commandeered someone's abandoned goods on Nastasinsky Lane, moved his wife and son to the prosperity of Paris in short order, and after earning himself a trip himself headed to Paris, where he had business: beaver, which had come into fashion in a major way that autumn; and another matter the direct opposite of beavers and their sale. Vasya was the principal element in this other matter, an element that not only concerned the personal relations between Kellerman and Gorbatov but also, in and of itself, given the chance, could be considered a public service in Moscow.

When Ilya rang the bell and a busty maid in a cap opened the door, he was asked who precisely he wished to see, Alexander Adolfovich or Adolf Alexandrovich?

"Alexander Adolfovich," Ilya said.

Cap in hand, he proceeded to the drawing room.

In that dark and most likely large apartment, where portraits of beauties and aged military men hung on the walls, where there were cabinets with secret locks in the partitions and, in the corners, curved sofas and love seats, there once must have lived people with an irreproachable past and moderate desires to whose fulfillment they had devoted their entire placid lives. In the nursery, as in the schoolroom pictures we all learned from once upon a time, children played; in the bedroom, adults slept; in the drawing room, guests sat; and in the dining room, servants passed steaming dishes. But in this perhaps too perfect life, something had happened that had forced them to allow strangers to sit on the Aubusson satins and under the Louis chandelier. Either monsieur had caught madame in the servant's embrace and demanded a divorce, or an old aunt had died leaving them an estate worth millions in Switzerland and it had been decided to resettle there posthaste, or a small child had fallen to the sidewalk of the decorous street while playing and the unhappy parents had lost all desire to stay on in this godforsaken place.

Ilya was left standing in the middle of the room.

Through three layers of lace curtains (small, large, and parted), he could see the apartment across the way: a white piano, a tall mirror, a silk comforter under a canopy that looked like the bed's gravy boat. There, monsieur had yet to catch madame in the servant's embrace, good Aunt Elise who had so many eccentricities had yet to die, and the curly-haired little girl had yet to fall from the tall window.

Ilya listened. People were walking around in the next room, a vacuum was running in a lower apartment, and the radio was emitting raspy cables:

"Hello . . . Hello . . . Rio Tinto . . . Chelles . . . Chelles . . . Royal Dutch . . . Hello . . ."

And a poor, timid Marseillaise could be heard as if from a child's music box.

When Ilya looked around, Alexander Adolfovich Kellerman was already in the room. He was standing in the doorway, arms and legs set wide, head tilted slightly to one side. The expression on his face was always the same: Yes, I'm cunning, but I beg you to note that I have decided not to conceal this fact from you.

He was wearing an excellent suit in a fine but colorful check with a soft, almost artistic collar, and a cheerful, expensive tie. His top trouser and bottom vest buttons were undone. He started toward Ilya.

"Hello, dear idealist!" he exclaimed, although, out of caution, not offering Ilya his hand. "I wasn't expecting you, but I'm glad, glad, believe me, and even somewhat flattered. Come in."

He made Ilya go into his study, himself followed, closed that door and another, one that evidently led to a hallway, and as he sat in an armchair by his desk, pulled up a comfortable leather chair for Ilya, amused at Ilya being unable to find a place for his cap.

It was immediately clear to Ilya that the person in front of him belonged to that category of people for whom time has a different dimension, another volume, than for the majority, to which he ascribed himself. These people were able to think about multiple things at once. The loving way Kellerman placed his short, puffy hand on the receiver of the telephone on his desk and with the other made a gesture graciously inviting Ilya to pull up his chair made it clear that no matter the fervor with which he had greeted Ilya, Kellerman had not forgotten his other affairs and quite possibly was even deciding them then and there.

"I said 'dear idealist,'" Kellerman began as soon as he felt, mistakenly, as it happened, that Ilya was about to speak, "but why 'dear' and why 'idealist'? 'Dear' because you are the son of our deeply esteemed Stepan Vasilievich, and 'idealist' . . . oh, don't ask me about that! That is so painful, I can't bear to think, let alone speak . . . Just think, what have you traded your youth for? But no, let's not get into that!"

He fell silent, having decided the time had come to hear out Ilya, but Ilya was following Kellerman silently and with curiosity.

"Allow me to be perfectly frank with you," he continued, with some impatience even, though not lifting his hand from the telephone. "My Adolf warned me that over the past few years you've filled your lungs with the excessively fresh fragrance of forests and fields, that in a certain sense you are now a child of nature and therefore there's no point in us counting on you. To what, in that case, do I owe your gracious visit?"

At that moment the telephone rang.

Still smiling, Kellerman lifted the receiver. The conversation was very brief: they'd called for Adolf, but Adolf wasn't there. When would he be? Oh, soon, by lunch, in all likelihood. Any message? No?

He replaced the receiver but kept his hand there.

"To what do I owe your gracious visit?" he repeated, his mind obviously elsewhere.

Ilya leaned toward him slightly.

"Alexander Adolfovich," he said with humble restraint, "leave Vasya alone."

Kellerman suddenly and very obviously snapped to. He felt the cards had been dealt and it was time to begin play immediately. Inspiration, a kind of shudder, pierced him, and he realized he'd been expecting these words, as he'd been expecting Ilya, but he decided not to let that show now.

He was still, but not for long. With his free hand he slapped his knee.

"By God, I never expected a request like that from you, Ilya Stepanovich!" he exclaimed with great good humor. "Am I really forcibly returning your Vasya to Stepan Vasilievich? Vasya's going of his own accord, so go talk to him. Even better, appeal to your dear papa. I'm merely carrying out his will, nothing more. I'm not forcing anyone."

Patiently, with a dogged courtesy and stamina, Ilya listened.

"Alexander Adolfovich," he spoke again. "This is why I came to Paris from the provinces. Leave Vasya alone."

"These kinds of humiliations are futile, Ilya Stepanovich, in front of someone with whom, if I'm not mistaken, you would not agree to shake hands. You shouldn't have left the provinces. Ha ha, forgive my rudeness. This has nothing to do with me."

"Here is your check," Ilya said, pulling the narrow, pale green paper out of his pocket. "Vasya is returning it to you."

Kellerman had not expected that, and an angry expression flitted across his face.

"Vasya asked me to tell you in person that he's made a decision," Ilya continued. "He wants to test himself in some way. He has no need of your money or the passport you get him. If he does decide to return to Russia, he'll do so without you. More than likely, he won't, but if he does then it won't be as a bought man, but at his own risk, and not to join Gorbatov but on his own. He asked me to tell you all this."

A grin flickered on Kellerman's lively lips.

"You must know," he said modestly, "that by doing this he is making trouble for me alone."

"Is that so? Why?" Ilya asked with animation. "Didn't you just say this had nothing to do with you?"

But Kellerman didn't see his mistake, and what did he care about slips of the tongue when in his mind a faultless plan for further action was mechanically taking precise shape? He barely understood that Ilya was laying a trap for him.

"I said"—and he made a vague gesture, not without elegance, it seemed to him—"I have no real role here. But you understand, my dear man, that in our day we come here not only to babble empty words about trade. We are now men of double, sometimes even triple professions. I don't need your Vasya, or rather, I alone don't. I need him in the third place; Stepan Vasilievich, of course, needs him in the second."

He suddenly fell silent, and again, as he weighed something, stared at Ilya, who didn't budge. Slowly, a big blue vein a finger thick swelled in the middle of his forehead.

"Actually, as always with us Russians, the practical aspects of something are linked in the subtlest way to a higher and mysterious meaning. Yes, yes; base, pocketbook objectives, shall we say, become wedded in our minds with an amazingly and sometimes headspinningly lofty justification. Forgive me, Ilya Stepanovich, but it seems to me that in this regard you've retained something of your lost homeland as well, am I right? Your idealism, which I apparently did not express myself about sufficiently brilliantly at the start of our conversation, is also linked to your so-called personal status, am I right? Actually, your youth might be easily insulted by this. I'm not about to compare myself to you, but I will say, since you've decided to stay a little longer, even though I decisively rejected your petition—I console myself with the fact that I'm going to be waging a true civil war with you."

Here was the word Ilya Gorbatov had come to the city of Paris from his provinces to hear!

"A war!" he exclaimed, and his eyes glittered. "I came to see you for that word: not Gorbatov's fatherly feelings, and not your friendship with him. You want to remove people from the land! And that is what Vasya means to you above all! You're starting your organized campaign against us with him—well, he is a tasty morsel, as you like. And it's been a major effort, after all—you've spent a year cultivating him. And this was his effort too, after all, the person flying into your flame himself, from whose soul time has lifted all bonds!"

Kellerman tilted his head toward his shoulder.

"I could never deny your cleverness," he said, thereby slowing the conversation's pace. "Back in

Patriarch Ponds you taught Vasya and my Adolf to sail toy boats. Only is there any point in getting worked up like this? What a bellicose youth, in fact! I dare say your Vasya is tying up his bundle right now and taking money out of Vera Kirillovna's bureau (what terrible childishness to return the check!). Vasya won't abandon us, we're starting with him."

Ilya stood up.

"Do you really think we'll give anyone up without a fight?" he said loudly and clearly, his broad palm leaning flat on Kellerman's desk. "Our people are not that kind. Oh, yes, you're perfectly right. For us the pocketbook interest is linked to a lofty goal, as it is with all Russians in general, we can't without that. But that is why this goal is secure, because it is freely combined with the pocketbook. The land is today's pocketbook for us, and it is leading toward meanings so lofty you can't even imagine them."

"I don't care, Ilya Stepanovich!" Kellerman threw up his hands. "It's nothing to do with me. Generally everything here with you is dreadfully complicated: a League of Nations, a Land Commission, and some other banality. We're simple people: get us a ticket and passport"— Alexander Adolfovich jokingly said "patchport"—"and that's that. And you know, he's lapping it up!"

Playfully, Kellerman swiveled his chair.

"You're the one who's lying, you scoundrel." Ilya said unexpectedly and with surprising calm. "Vasya's the first bite now, but he's the pledge of your future work here and that's why you need him so badly. Gorbatov will see to it that you get a big promotion for him, that's clear."

"I'm asking you to leave now," Kellerman said. "Thank you for 'scoundrel.' I took it with ordinary interest."

Ilya looked at him with amazement.

"What scum!" he said, a little naïvely. "Yes, it truly is wrong to let anyone go that low."

He picked up his cap, which he'd managed to stick behind the chess table at one point. Kellerman followed him silently.

And at that moment, Ilya felt like tossing out something foolish, something cheap and silly. He stood in the middle of the room and sensed that no one would ever find out the absurd thing he was dying to say. He would never have to blush for this; no one would shame him. He couldn't be ashamed of himself; he didn't care about himself, he still didn't know how to judge himself and didn't much believe that it was even possible, considered it hypocrisy. Moreover, he hoped that with time this childishness he couldn't resist, that drew him with its simplicity, would depart from memory.

"Comrade Kellerman, button your trousers," he said, just as if he'd slid to the bottom of a hill. He immediately felt light and cheerful. He walked quickly to the foyer, felt for the lock on the front door, and opened it. But here another meeting awaited him, actually not all that unexpected: on the landing, slamming the elevator doors, stood Adolf.

Ilya had a hard time believing it was him. His broad hips looked vast because of the checkered trousers that fell to his fat ankles, and his immobile face as ever held nothing remarkable: his light eyes, which he had lately begun to hide behind large, smoky eyeglasses, and his large, flat mouth were and somehow were not the same. Over the last four years he had coarsened and bulked up uncommonly. He saw Ilya and actually shuddered with surprise; as a child he was long treated for excessive impressionability, primarily with gymnastics and grapes. Ilya stopped ingenuously.

But a few moments passed and he suddenly remembered there was no point standing here, and also he'd left the door to the Kellermans' apartment wide open. He walked across the landing with his usual step, such as, for example, the way he would walk from the barn to the house and back, and started going down the stairs, as if he were going down from the attic to the kitchen, to join Marianna. At that moment Adolf turned to follow him.

"Where are you staying?" he asked hoarsely, maintaining all his dignity, or so he thought.

"Why do you care?"

"Tell me, you won't regret it. Wait a minute. Where are you going? Leave me your address."

He seemed in a state of uncharacteristic alarm, and Ilya stopped. He looked at the broad, polished railings leading down.

"Fourteen, rue Ganneron," he said. Why shouldn't he tell him his address?

It was abundantly clear that Adolf had been expecting that answer. Otherwise, why should he be so worried?

"The Hôtel Celtique!" he exclaimed, leaning over the railing, as if he were afraid Ilya might not hear (in that time, Ilya had reached the lower landing). "I have a friend living there, a girl. Actually, she's nearly thirty, that girl. Nowadays everyone's a girl."

Wasn't this too much? Downstairs, the front door was crowded with unwieldy windows and iron gratings, and Adolf entered his apartment as if nothing at all had happened.

CHAPTER FIVE

I LYA WAS HUNGRY. The lilac air, heavy with humidity and the city's exhalations, first came toward him with the wind, then rested on his shoulders with all the still dampness collected from the stone streets. It was just past noon. There weren't any restaurants in these wealthy areas, and even if there had been, Ilya wouldn't have had the nerve to go in. He didn't know where exactly he was going to have breakfast. Best would be to go back to the Place Clichy and eat cheaply there, somewhere near his building. And that is what he did.

At last, everything had been illuminated. He hadn't told Shaibin a single lie. He had not had any real hope that Kellerman would give up on Vasya. Ilya was glad they hadn't even gone as far as negotiating that. They hadn't argued, hadn't demanded concessions from each other in the name of Stepan Vasilievich's fatherly feelings. About Vasya, the son regarding whom his father had certain rights, not a single word had been said, basically. Kellerman himself had shifted the conversation to a different plane, a political plane. And that was good.

Ilya Gorbatov had not left his Provençal farm to straighten out family affairs. For a long time people had been writing to him, saying that there was regular work underway in Paris among the people awaiting land—cautious work, clandestine work—and Ilya had long realized that Adolf and his father were mixed up in this work, that catching Vasya would be an auspicious beginning for their activities, but no proof of this had penetrated to the distant Vaucluse.

There was something Ilya believed in, and that was Vasya's automatic honesty. Half an hour before Ilya's departure for Paris, Vasya had managed to give him the check and say the same thing—but disjointedly and hastily—that Ilya told Kellerman. All that remained was to rush home and assure him of the arrangement. To be the means for Kellerman's sinister purposes—no, Vasya couldn't do that. So thought Ilya.

Meanwhile, he went into a restaurant.

They cleared a table for him in the corner, by the window, where through the gap in the soiled curtain he could see the sidewalk and a narrow strip of street.

Next to him, in the fumes from the kitchen nearby, a young woman and a worker were focused on their breakfast, wiping their plates from time to time with their bread.

For them, this was ordinary; for Ilya, a strange, joyless holiday. He was in the city and a little drunk from the noise and the shortage of air. What was the sky like today? He hadn't seen it yet. The day was humid and windy, the kind of day there could be too many of in autumn, especially in October. Ilya didn't know them.

He asked for potatoes in vinegar and a steak, but well done; it's hard for country people to eat bloody meat. After he ate the steak, he ordered another—and his neighbors looked at him amiably and respectfully. Then they served him cheese and dessert. He treated his neighbors to wine.

He still had two more places to go, but he decided to put off both matters until tomorrow. Tomorrow was Sunday; he'd be able to get there and back and see the people he needed to see. Right now he was very tired. The past two nights he'd slept unforgivably little, and the last night in the train car Shaibin had prevented all sleep. Ilya didn't know what to think of Shaibin, yet he had the feeling the hardest part was behind him.

When he got to his room he opened his suitcase— and on top lay Marianna's note: "Ilyusha! Bring me a present of lilac soap, the kind they wash with in Paris." He scattered his undershirt, razor, soap, hankies, and brush, took off his jacket and shoes, and collapsed on the bed. And only then, over the roof of the building opposite, did he see an edge of sky: the rim of a perfectly still, smoky cloud. Ilya fell asleep instantly.

He didn't move for two, maybe three hours. It was growing gray and dusky in the room, and the light outside was weakening. Ilya was lying on his back, his mouth half open, his arms outstretched, and at the opposite end of the bed his feet poked out in their gray striped socks. The woman who had come in without knocking and was sitting by the table had looked at them for a long time, then rummaged in his jacket pockets, found matches, and lit a cigarette.

She sat for a long time. The water groaned in the pipes; it was getting dark; the street would quiet down and then a truck would race down it, making the building shake. The woman could see herself in the armoire mirror, and this entertained her. She was wearing the same dark dress and brown shoes as that morning. She had time to count the rows of faded flowers on the wallpaper and reread Marianna's note. She sat and smoked but would not have woken Ilya for anything in the world.

First of all, she had no specific engagements, and she was free to sit like this until evening. In the evenings, or rather nights, she was busy: she performed at a nightclub, the Palais des Boyards. She and her partner Lyosha danced the Sicilian tango, and she wore a black dress covered to the chin in front and with a bare back. Lyosha had dislocated her pinky out of contempt—that was the extent of their relationship. Lyosha would be driven by Americans or Germans (but who could tell just by looking) to secret dens or led away to the nearest hotel. And Lyosha was getting rich. People said he was saving up, that he wanted to bring his mother to Paris from Zhizdra.

Nyusha would dance her Sicilian tango. If she'd tried to she could have danced something else, or even sung. Afterward, she would take off the black dress, put on another with sleeves, and sell dolls, which she would carry between the tables in a large flat basket; they had long, limp arms, brocade dresses, and faces painted by Mr. Rastoropenko in his workshop (although people said he was going broke). People laughed at Nyusha at the Palais des Boyards and in other places: the Troika, the Cavo, and the Usadebka. When she arrived at the Zanzibar for dinner, they told her she was lowering herself and soon would no longer be able to consider herself an artist. People were surprised at her for another reason too: at the night-club she never sat with anyone, she just did her job.

She would arrive at the Zanzibar just before two, after the nightclub closed. Here she would wait for Berta, Natasha, and Merichka, who would come from very different places—Natasha straight off the street; lately her affairs had been quite wretched. Here they would have their dinner. Here redheaded Henri would run for them from salad to mustard, let the cup clatter on its saucer, and, dangling his elbow, pour coffee in a ruddy stream, with his other hand bringing a lighter to someone's dying cigarette. Here Nyusha would spend an hour or two before heading for the Hôtel Celtique. And here, often, her soul would be uneasy: weeks would pass, letters would come from Africa, letters would come from Provence, Adolf Kellerman would write her notes. Life was passing.

Nyusha sat in a thick haze: the smoke of three cigarettes hung in the air. It was dark outside. Without turning on the light, she walked to the bed and leaned over Ilya. Only then did he open his eyes.

"Hello, Ilya," she said, distraught.

He took her hand, moved closer, forced her to sit and then to lie down beside him.

"Have you been waiting long?" he asked, peering into her face, dark against the white pillow.

"Yes."

"Why didn't you wake me?"

Not knowing what to say, she closed her eyes, and wordlessly, tenderly, he ran his hand over her shoulder and hip. She made an effort not to stir. He touched her hair, smooth at the forehead and gathered at the nape; neither one could get a word out. They lay in that unstuffy, loose embrace for a long time, and their breathing warmed their faces.

Nyusha said, "I'm going to kiss you, Ilya, I'm so happy to see you."

She stretched toward him and kissed him on the forehead and eyes, and he kissed her hand. She gazed at him radiantly, and in the twilight she saw his broad face, which to her looked made of stone; only his eyes flashed brightly, keenly.

"Do you want to go away with me the day after tomorrow?" he asked.

"As your wife? Your lover?"

"No."

"I can't," she said, pressing her face to his broad chest, "I can't lie to you. I don't have the strength to go."

He looked over her at his scattered things, which— look at that!—had turned up with him here in Paris. He looked without blinking until his eyes got tired.

"Shall I turn on the light?" he asked.

"Don't."

She smelled like apricots to him. She lay with her knees slightly bent, and seemed to be warming her hands right at his heart.

"Why is it so good to be silent with you, Ilya?" she said, not expecting an answer. "You're one big 'why' for me"—and she smiled at how that had come out. "Why don't you love me? Why don't you love anyone? Don't answer, I love you most when you don't say anything."

She cautiously turned her head away from his chest and looked into his face. Slowly she reached out and put her arm around his neck.

"Where are you asking me to go? Where are you asking me to go without you, my dear friend?" she said with tenderness, and instantly tears filled her eyes. "Do you really think I can live alongside you and not suffer? Do you really think I can live on my own and not be lost? Who can live on their own and not be lost? Among us—no one."

"Among you?"

"Among us—us lasts. And if someone doesn't want to be lost, Ilya (and sometimes one doesn't), that person immediately searches for a hand . . . Give me your hand."

Ilya pressed her limp, slightly damp hand.

"You're not callous, you're not cold, so why don't you love me? Look inside me for one minute: there, I want to be saved, I want to be saved by love, I found you. But you . . . How old are you?"

"Twenty-five."

"Yes. That's not very old. That's why I can be so frank with you. I like it that you can't compare me to anyone, it makes me feel a little proud, that illusion that I'm your one and only, when in fact I'm not yours in any way. Don't you find it silly that you and I are lying in the dark? That I have my arms around you? You wanted to turn on the light, I think."

"No, leave it."

"How surprised your people would be if I were to come. Your stepmother wouldn't let me in."

"She asked me whether to expect you."

Nyusha pushed back a little.

"You're lying."

"I'm telling the truth. She thought I was going to bring you."

"She doesn't hate me? She doesn't . . . Forgive me, Ilya, I thought she felt it was all my fault."

"It's not your fault Shaibin loves you."

Nyusha leaned back, let go of Ilya's neck, and covered her face with her hand. The white of her lace cuff contrasted with the darkness.

"How you said that!" she exclaimed in anguish. "It's all my fault, all my fault. His three years in Africa, my sister's death—that's all on my conscience. And other things, lots of other things. Why should you know? You pity me as it is."

She glanced at him again and saw his slightly parted lips.

"You have to get away from here," Ilya whispered, catching her eye.

She grinned bitterly.

"And go where? There's probably not even a hairdresser where you are. Who's going to cut my hair?"

She thrashed around on the wide bed, both hands flung over her head.

"I can't leave and I can't stay. Do you understand?" she said, with a sudden callousness in her voice. "Living is impossible for me. I want to live, I want to save myself, but it turns out I have nowhere to go."

Ilya impulsively squeezed both her hands in one of his.

"Don't you dare! Be quiet! Don't you dare speak that way!" he said forcefully, leaning over her. "If you dare say that one more time! Do you even understand what you're saying? Listen to me. You're leaving here. Time will pass, maybe even a very short time, and your life will change. You're afraid of your destiny. Do you know what destiny is? Everyone around you is afraid of their destiny, but they will stop being afraid, they will! Trust me—you used to trust me in everything, or am I wrong? All this will change, all this will pass. You have no idea how much yet. Only don't look for help. It's not other people who are going to save you—you're going to save yourself, if only you can find the will, and maybe someone else can come to life through you too. My poor darling, how I wish you trusted me!"

She was helplessly silent.

"So I'm supposed to trust you?" she whispered, opening her eyes and staring into space. "But why? Why? Do you really not know everything? You took away my hope. Imagine, until today I still hoped, we all still hope, we can't understand anything properly from letters. You're not offering me love."

Again she brought her face close to his.

"And now you want me to trust you."

She leaned forward slowly and, giving him time to make the slightest, most imperceptible movement, which she couldn't help but sense, kissed him on the lips tenderly, chastely. He closed his eyes.

"Never, with anyone?" she asked quietly.

"Never."

"But how is that possible?"

"Nyusha, darling, what are you asking? How do I know? It's just—it hasn't happened, not really—the desire hasn't been there. How can I know? Maybe I'm a freak, a cripple, I don't know. Forgive me."

She slipped off the bed, turned on the light, and was drawn to the mirror. She looked into her own eyes with alarm and shame.

"What did you tell your stepmother when she asked about me?" she said, not looking in the direction of the bed.

"I said you wouldn't come."

"Why did you just ask me to?"

"I could have been wrong, but as you see, I wasn't."

"You weren't wrong again? So you're saying I'm going to save myself?"

"You're absolutely going to save yourself."

"Lord, let him not be wrong this time, and have mercy on me!" Nyusha said, and she crossed herself and bowed.

Ilya remained lying there; he rubbed his face against the pillow, which smelled of apricots.

"What are you and I going to do this evening?" Nyusha asked.

"We're going to have supper together," he said, "and then we'll go for a walk . . . to some garden."

"The gardens are closed, and the weather's wrong."

She walked up to him; the tip of a feather, the kind pillows are usually stuffed with, poked out of the thick, coarse pillowcase. She plucked it; Ilya watched her fingers without moving.

"When you were a child, in your bed (mine had an iron grill at either end), did you ever feel for these sharp little tips? You're excited, you pull it out, and suddenly, unexpectedly, a wonderful, beautiful little feather, from who knows where, from the old mattress, comes out into the light of day. Did you ever?"

She pulled and a smooth, gray feather did indeed emerge from the pillow.

"It did, and just like that," Nyusha said, and she smiled. Ilya smiled too. "Well, I'm going to get dressed. Be ready. We'll get supper."

She went out. The clock downstairs struck seven. Ilya heard Nyusha's steps above him, and then everything fell quiet. And then he was flooded with the same thoughts, the same feelings, that had lived inside him half unconsciously for the past few hours. He closed his eyes.

His eyelids were hot. He picked up the feather Nyusha had dropped and ran it over his eyes. It was as if someone were touching his eyelids with her silky lashes. "Mama," he said aloud. And it was all over. He jumped up, put on his shoes, smoothed his hair.

This evening of the 22nd of September passed into dream in Ilya's memory. Very little of it stuck: Nyusha's sad eyes as she sat across from him in a small, noisy restaurant, their taciturn supper. The chill of the streets, the gleam of the lights; her feminine hand in his hand (he never wore gloves); and, finally, the magician. Whether they were at a circus or a street fair, he couldn't quite tell. The magician created his wonders three steps away from Ilya—he came right down into the audience. Later, that night, this magician came to him and continued to turn water into wine.

"Our Lord Jesus Christ Himself couldn't have done better," he kept repeating.

But that night this was real sleep, the kind he and Vasya usually slept: deep, unmoving, unheard. There had been a Japanese child at the street fair too. He was six years old and was wearing pink trousers that gradually soaked through in front as the little boy did his intricate acrobatics. It ended with the boy being carried away: there was a puddle under the trapeze.

Nyusha laughed and even cried a little. They went home arm in arm. It was eleven o'clock, time for Nyusha to go to her nightclub and dance her Sicilian tango.

He hoped this melancholy evening with Nyusha would pass into dream! He hoped that now, in hardworking Provence, where the land so loved the human hand, he would no longer remember whether Nyusha wept or laughed when she walked away from his door, number 34; Ilya hoped that in fifty years, when the mysterious human memory suddenly made everything that happened in our obscure youth clear again, he would not remember these cold evening hours! But he hoped that, both now and in fifty years (he was probably going to live a very long time), he would not forget that fresh Sunday morning and his encounters—planned and not—in a certain corner of Paris. Not that he could, they were impossible to forget! Anyone who had once been there, who had once seen them, would keep in his heart forever, if only secretly, a memory that had no equal in the world for injury and pain. And Ilya Gorbatov hoped that in his mature years of struggle and insight the thought of that September morning would pass before him and pierce him with its point; and in his old age, when other memories approached, memories of a complexly and passionately lived life, and tried to cloud the dream of that bitter outing—they wouldn't be able to! Oh, may you have grandchildren, Ilya, so that you can tell them the story, so this reality can be conveyed to their hearts. Gather your great-grandchildren around, and let them hear the tale more terrible than the tale of Bluebeard, more terrible than all the tales there have ever been on earth, a tale that perhaps they are not yet of an age to be told. And when you begin to dream of the grave, and out of your old man's helplessness you feel an urge to find those who also wandered these dark places on their outings, may the word "Paris" be a watchword for you who survived with a decayed heart ... May it all remain in your heart: dying Pashka's every word, and Mr. Rastoropenko's mother, and that very same Pyotr Ivanovich who was standing closer to the door. Anyone who hasn't seen it—he won't believe your story, Ilya, and even Vera Kirillovna herself, now tossed to foreign lands, even she herself won't believe you. To the whole world, this will sound like a fairy tale.

The morning was fresh and overcast; the shredded clouds made the heights tiresomely gaudy; people flashed by, automobiles circulated; the wind came off the Channel in gusts and curled the branches of the beggared plane trees; the boulevards receded down a luxurious curve into the dove-gray expanse.

Ilya went out at about nine and set off on foot across the city to where "ours" lived. He missed physical movement: the sidewalks' stone could not tire his sturdy legs sufficiently.

"Ours" lived, as befitted them, in the most diverse parts of Paris (to say nothing of the suburbs); those Ilya was going to see had settled not too far from the best parts of the capital: the military school, the Champ de Mars. Actually, the Champ de Mars wasn't all that close, half an hour's walk or more. Here the slums, in the full sense of the word, began, and rather abruptly.

First came primarily commercial streets— commerce almost exclusively in food and footwear. Hawkers' trays buckled under apples, and felt slippers had been brought out from the buildings nearly to the street. Commerce was more boisterous here on holidays than weekdays; rambunctious crowds roamed right down the street, not knowing how to kill the time. Then came much quieter, cobbled streets with peeling two-story buildings, wooden gates that had a spigot sticking out alongside. After these streets, fairly unseemly for Paris, began the quiet, deserted dead ends.

The buzz and roar of engines didn't reach here; here there was poverty—and the cloud over it. The windows, evidently long unwashed, did not have curtains, but you couldn't make out anything in them anyway, which was probably for the best. Why should people look at each other? A cat big with young dashed from gate to gate. Ilya stopped and checked the building number. There was a handcart in the street, heaped with holey straw chairs.

Yes, this was the right building. Through the gate was the door to the City of Kiev tavern, and next to the narrow, well-fingerprinted door was a large zinc bucket full of garbage. Piled next to that was everything that hadn't fit into it: rust-red ash, a bouquet of withered flowers, empty tin cans, and various other objects Ilya couldn't identify. Bending over this pile, over this stench of rotting carnations, were a skinny girl of nine or so and a somewhat younger boy. Both were silently digging through the dubious objects.

The girl managed to cut herself on a can and patiently sucked her bloodied finger; the boy observed keenly to see whether he, too, might want anything she pulled out.

"Why are you here?" Ilya asked, and cold sweat appeared on his forehead and neck.

The girl raised her shy, hungry eyes to him. Her hair was plaited into two even braids, but she was dressed badly and dirtily.

"We're looking for flowers," she said slyly, and went back to her interrupted work. The boy didn't even look at Ilya.

Yes, this was the right building.

The City of Kiev's swarthy cook suddenly flung the door open—in the cramped kitchen Ilya glimpsed in that moment, the burned fat made it hard to breathe. The cook furiously shook a net of salad greens, and the spray flew in all directions.

"Get out of here, you gnats!" he shouted, and the children barely managed to raise their heads when a whole handful of potato peels flew past. The children fell on them instantly.

Ilya went on.

A narrow courtyard, unevenly paved, as a result of which a shiny, watery damp had collected here and there; on one side, a long, one-story annex, and on the other an old brickwork wall; straight ahead, in the cramped back of the courtyard, a covered latrine and beside it an awning over a man who had spread a newspaper under himself and was repairing the woven seat of a dilapidated chair. Apparently the handcart left on the street belonged to him.

But Ilya didn't approach him right away. He walked slowly past the annex windows. People here lived not only on the first floor but also in the basement, the windows of which were even with the ground, and when you looked through them you could see a rutted stone floor and a few stray pieces of ramshackle furniture. There, at one of the windows, a broken window, his nose pressed to its sharp edges, squatting, was a small, fair-haired boy, stock-still. He was staring down through the window to where, far back in the low, empty room, in the corner, a boy of about seven, on a thin mattress covered with an old soldier's greatcoat, a boy of about seven just like him, was lying on his back with wide-open eyes.

He lay without moving and also refused to turn his big, inflamed eyes away from the window. Everything indicated that he had a fever, and a high one. His lips were parted and released a faint steam and a brief rasp; his hair was stuck together—his forehead was bathed in sweat!

The boy at the window finally took his hand cautiously out of the pocket of his ratty jacket. A broken penknife gleamed in his hand.

"Pashka, hey, Pashka! I've got a penknife," he said, as if he were starting a game, dying of curiosity.

Pashka stirred under the greatcoat; anguish contorted his thin little face.

"Gimme!" he said quietly, and he opened his dark eyes even wider. The boy at the window laughed.

"And when you die, who's going to give it back to me?" he asked greedily.

"Papa will," Pashka's weak voice reached him.

"No he won't. Better I play with it a little, and when you die I'll put it in your coffin."

A shadow of hope passed through Pashka's eyes, and he attempted a smile.

"No lie?"

"Cross my heart!"

"Don't lie. Otherwise I'll come back from the next world and scare you, hear me?"

So many words finally wore him out. For a few moments he tossed under the greatcoat and then he fell still.

"Who's that?" Ilya asked.

"It's Pashka," the boy replied, not taking his concerned gaze from the window.

And Ilya went on.

Women were sewing in a window; one was still young and didn't look up when he stopped. The old woman set aside her work, worry in her eyes.

"Where can I find Rastoropenko here?" Ilya shouted so they could hear him through the window.

"Keep going, keep going"—and the old woman waved him on. Farther along was the low door to a cobbler's shop. Here, his back to the cobbler, sat a man wearing a medal who was tinkering with a disassembled clock. "Enough already. Isn't it Sunday today?" Truth be told, the cobbler didn't care. He was pounding the heel of a lady's boot worn to the nails with a hard despair.

"We're closed today," the man with the medal said.

"Does anyone know where Rastoropenko lives?"

"They do." And the man repeated, "They certainly do."

He rose from his stool, put down the clock, and, weight in hand, went to the door to show Ilya how to get to the right apartment. But right then the cobbler suddenly stopped pounding and squinted at Ilya.

"If you're here about floor polishing, they don't do that anymore," the man with the medal said as he reached the door.

"No, I'm from the provinces."

"You mean you're here about our travel?" the cobbler asked suddenly, timidly, letting the nails drop from his mouth.

Ilya nodded silently. Both looked at him for a minute in embarrassed astonishment.

"You came yourself?" they began disjointedly and at once. "You mean it's soon? And they'll pay for our travel?"

Ilya nodded again.

"Yes. I need to see one of the Rastoropenkos. Can you take me there?"

"Sure we can take you to the Rastoropenkos, why not." The cobbler began to fuss. "How is it I didn't recognize you, eh? No, tell us, please, what a coincidence!"

The man with the medal was more reserved; he took Ilya by the sleeve and hurried him through the courtyard.

"From the provinces! My, what a word! We've forgotten that word," he mumbled.

The furniture repairer under the awning joined them. On the steep stairs with the iron railings, it seemed to Ilya at least five people had gathered behind him already.

"Pashka, hey, Pashka, I've got a penknife," he heard from the courtyard.

Mr. Rastoropenko's apartment consisted of one very narrow, long, and dirty room where the only furniture was a wide ottoman sunken at one end, a table, and two chairs—Mr. Rastoropenko's dear mama was sleeping on the floor. Nonetheless, it was fairly hard to enter the room because wires were stretched crosswise, at the height of a man's face, and hanging on those wires with a pedantic and even somewhat exaggerated painstakingness were painted doll heads on wire hooks, about seventy of them, all smiling sadly. You couldn't see anything around these rather tastelessly made and supremely poignant objects. There was gold powder flying around the room, like sun glints, and the smell of turpentine. Rastoropenko, as they had correctly told Ilya, no longer polished floors. He and his wife and mother had temporarily begun a new and equally unprofitable business.

"Bend way down so you don't touch anything, God forbid," came Rastoropenko's mama's voice. She couldn't see who exactly had come in but guessed from all the signs that it was several people at once. Rastoropenko's wife, Marina Petrovna, a tall woman with hair piled high, on the heavy side and swarthy, bending neatly as needed, suddenly appeared two paces away from Ilya.

"I'm Gorbatov," he said, removing his cap.

She blushed thickly and slowly, the way people with swarthy skin blush. She gave Ilya and the people who had come in with him a swift once-over.

"Gorbatov ... Come in ... Sit down ..." Flustered, she moved the doll heads on the wire aside and let Ilya pass. A few entered behind him; on the stairs, even more people seemed to have come up.

Marina Petrovna waited for Ilya to sit down while she herself sat in the middle of the room—but this time she wasn't embarrassed.

"This is how we live, you see," she blurted out, somewhat hysterically. "Did you see the courtyard? There are children ... Better there weren't!"

She spoke with him as with a stranger; she was ashamed of something.

"I came by to say that you can pack up at the end of this week," Ilya said. "I'm going home tomorrow, and you'll have your travel money sent to you immediately. The matter has been settled, as I wrote, but I came to warn you all to be ready."

And at that moment he looked up and saw them all. They were "ours," assembled from all over the courtyard. There was an entire crowd standing in the doorway, at least ten people.

They gave way a little—and Mr. Rastoropenko squeezed into the room.

"Ilya Stepanovich, my dear man, forgive the upheaval," he said. Whether he was apologizing for his own upheaval or for the general, disorderly but quiet upheaval of "ours" was unclear.

He exchanged greetings with Ilya. They knew each other well, though they had never seen each other before. However, the prolonged matter of resettling the Rastoropenkos on the land that Ilya was seeing to in Saint-Didier and their steady correspondence had fortified their straightforward relations. They barely gave themselves time to examine each other.

"Did you hear what he said?" Marina Petrovna exclaimed. "We're going. Did you hear?"

The people fluttered up. The old mama was gathering up the dolls. God forbid they spoil them! Behind the wire he could now see the pale (truly, why were they always so pale?) faces.

"How's about clothes?" someone's voice rang out.

"If anyone doesn't have clothing, you can take care of that there, that's not hard," Ilya said. "At first they'll give you everything, even fuel. It's a new business, and these Frenchmen are very generous."

"It's thanks to you, Ilya Stepanovich, their generosity," Rastoropenko put in. "You think we don't know?"

"Maybe benefactors of some kind?" another voice asked.

"No, not benefactors. They're spending now but they'll take their due later. As I wrote, it's a matter of the future. Also, the local agricultural credit funds will help you out."

Those in back started crowding those in front.

"The factory workers should stop pushing," the mama said. "Factory workers are always pushing everyone around."

Among those who came in were the two women who'd been sewing by the window. All the men had come—as if straight from work. No one was wearing their holiday best, as they say. Actually, half hadn't had any work for a long time.

"Here's what I was wondering: there are craftsmen among you, after all, so you'll have to abandon your craft temporarily. Temporarily, because later, maybe in a few years if things keep going like this, a Russian village will be set up. Right now there's feverish work underway aimed at gathering people—everyone's so scattered. Later there'll be work for Russian crafts-men. But right now, everyone's going to have to work on the land."

The cobbler, whose name was Pyotr Ivanovich, was standing closest to Ilya.

"That's what we've agreed to!" he exclaimed. "God knows I won't miss my trade! I only took it on by chance anyway. Most of our nomad camp didn't get started young, but due to misfortune."

"I also meant to say that you have hard work ahead of you. All in all, as you maybe know, the fact that you're turning your proletarian selves into peasants is unnatural. It's going in reverse. The opposite process is considered natural: right now people are moving from the countryside to the city. That means there's a certain difficulty, organic almost, at the very root of your resettlement. Do you understand?"

The people were standing stock-still in front of him; Rastoropenko addressed both them and Ilya at the same time.

NINA BERBEROVA

"That means we're taking the reverse path, the opposite path, to all Europe's astonishment, as it were."

"Life is in work. We've learned, we're not afraid," someone said.

"It's grueling labor, as I wrote," Ilya went on. "You won't be landowners right away. Your work is going to be sort of transitional. You'll live the way the peasants there live; you'll have chickens and rabbits: you'll work on the asparagus, and there's a canning factory there. There can't be any initiative until you save up enough, which you can do in a few years—and then it will be good, then you'll be closer to tenancy. Only there'll be no pleasures or entertainment."

Marina Petrovna, all worked up, with burning eyes and feverish hands, interrupted him:

"What pleasures do we have here? Can you tell me that? The cinema and bed, and the cinema is pure poison . . . And bed . . . what good is it when there's nothing you can do for your children, when you shouldn't be having children. For a Russian woman a bed without children is no pleasure!" She was burning up and tears were welling in her eyes. Everyone looked down, and Rastoropenko made signs to her that she either didn't see or didn't want to.

"It's hard for children there," Ilya began again. "There's no school, no proper teaching. Once you

133

move, my stepmother wants to start a traveling school, but right now things are bad—you'll just be looking after your cows."

A man, bearded and pale, stepped out from the back rows. It was getting hard to breathe in the room because of the people who had gradually arrived to stand around Ilya and Mr. Rastoropenko.

"And what, dear man, do our children face here, do you know?" asked the bearded man, and his lips trembled. "We have no money to teach them; we have to scrimp every kopek. Tend your cows—goodness me! Here they can look forward to dying in the street, there's tuberculosis here. God have mercy!"

Rastoropenko, agitated, spoke up:

"You know it yourself, Ilya Stepanovich, and it's only because you're so sincerely scrupulous that you want to warn us of all this. Two months ago you yourself took a little girl out of this very house, just with your letter."

Ilya was embarrassed.

"She's traveling now," he said quietly.

"With him?"

"With him."

"And how is he doing?"

"Poorly. We saw each other recently."

People gradually moved away from the door. Also here were the cook from the City of Kiev and the man who'd been repairing chairs, who turned out to be legless. They were craning their necks in Ilya's direction, but Ilya was flustered. He definitely didn't know what to tell them; he wasn't accustomed to speaking and he'd already written so much to them about everything!

"Here we are talking about children. Family is the main thing on the land. If there's a woman in the home, things go differently; if there's an older one, things go much better. Rumor has it that the Cossacks in the Pyrénées are suffering mightily from a lack of womenfolk. They have invalids instead of women washing dishes and mending shirts."

Someone smiled; Ilya himself had nothing against ending with a joke. But right then someone was noisily running up the stairs.

"Mama!" a child's voice cried out behind the people standing there, and there was such misery, such fear in that cry that the people by the door parted. Between the two columns, Ilya saw a boy holding a penknife, the same boy who'd just been standing by the window. He was so pale, it seemed he might be sick any minute, or might faint. He stood on the threshold for an instant and then suddenly, with a long, piercing wail, rushed toward Marina Petrovna, convulsing.

"Pashka's gone!" he shouted, and he thrashed in her arms. Everyone rushed outside.

Marina Petrovna splashed cold water on her son's face, bringing the boy around from his sobbing, and tucked him in on the ottoman. Mr. Rastoropenko's mama crossed herself and began hanging the dolls up again.

Ilya rose to his feet. In the general confusion no one tried to detain him, not that there was any point in saying goodbye—in less than a week he would see them on the fields of faraway Provence. True, he spoke with Rastoropenko on the stairs for another fifteen minutes. The travel funds would come in Rastoropenko's name. Oh! He nearly forgot: tell everyone they'll be insured there.

The curious were crowding into the courtyard; the small basement door was ajar. Who there was grieving over Pashka's body? His father? His mother? So far no one, so far women, strangers, were busying themselves there. He hadn't had a mother, and his father wasn't expected home before nightfall.

A few people said goodbye to Ilya; Pyotr Ivanovich, the cobbler, asked him for a cigarette. In the wind he caught the match's flame in Ilya's hand. And once again the deserted dead end, the street, and another street stretched out. Once again people were making noise, scurrying in and out, and once again Ilya walked across the entire city.

The time has come to describe his visit to a certain public figure.

The person we have decided to refer to only as the Advocate, due to the fact that he still lives and functions among us, lived in a small, tidy apartment near the Parc Monceau, furnished back before the war, during the days when the Advocate himself was deported from Russia for the 1905 revolution. He was a bachelor and lived with a sister ten years his elder. He had books and he had a dog, and within these walls, where Viktor Chernov once squinted and Savinkov nervously straightened his cuffs, the Advocate felt calm and lucid. True, lately, especially when he looked out the window at the park fence and the perambulators behind it, he did experience a certain unease. He didn't quite understand what exactly was going on with him. Speaking for ourselves, there were three reasons for his unease: Freemasonry, his digestion, and the settlement of Russian refugees on French land.

Let's set the first two reasons aside. The Advocate's digestion wasn't all that good, of course, but at fifty many have significantly worse. Nor is this the place to bring up Freemasonry, which does not concern us either. We'll say only that lately the Advocate had pulled back from it a little. Whether for good or ill, we don't know, and speculation on the topic is a futile business.

As for the settlement of Russian refugees on French land, he had taken this up suddenly, taken it up with his whole, most noble heart. He had traveled to Toulouse *comme un prostoi moujik*, like a common man—had walked from Cossack farm to Cossack farm, in the summer had been in Provence (he couldn't stand Provence for the most part and preferred Switzerland to everything else) and there had come upon Ilya, who suddenly taught him a certain jealousy. He became jealous of Canada and Argentina over the Russian grain-growers (some of whom had gone there to settle on the land also); he had cultivated the acquaintance of an influential member of parliament, a leftist, or rather, revived it and had taken part in the activities of the Land Commission created in Paris back in 1926.

The Advocate looked like a Russian intellectual, that is, someone of mixed blood. He was thin, his beard was much lighter than his mustache, and his mustache was lighter than his hair, itself sparse and slightly disheveled. Unusual vitality and passion lived in his irregular and even simply deformed fingers. He might—not in the least embarrassed by his interlocutor, in front of everyone—twist a finger in his nose or ear, but truth be told he was extraordinarily loved. And rightly so: there was something incredibly pleasant about him.

During his sojourn in Provence he became close to Ilya in just a few hours, thanks to their fervent and unusually sincere conversation; he realized that Ilya appreciated both his unfailing pleasantness and his most noble heart. For him, Ilya turned out to be "substantive proof" of his theory. No one yet knew about this theory other than the Advocate's elderly sister. The theory was the fruit of his admittedly somewhat idle imagination; the Advocate wanted no matter what for this theory to give a somewhat poetic answer to the questions raised by 1917, as he used to put it. For him, substantive proofs were essential.

Parting with Ilya after their first meeting and feeling a kind of infatuation for him, an infatuation, actually, that quite often gripped him after parting with an acquaintance, he made Ilya promise to pay him a visit the very next time he came to Paris. Ilya himself had no idea what captivated him about this tall, bony man. He even asked himself this question as he was ringing at the Advocate's door but could find no answer other than that he always felt a tenderness for the breed of unique people—among whom he justly included the chance Provençal summer visitor.

As far as the Advocate was concerned, there was no Moscow swindler Stepan Vasilievich, no Vasya lost in the sublunar realm. He knew only Ilya and called him by his last name, indifferent to his first, picturing him as an attractive, independent unit, abstractly and optimistically. He brought Ilya into a room that had a narrow bed covered with a piqué blanket, bookshelves lining the walls, and a desk by the window. A large Newfoundland lay in front of the hot fireplace beating its tail languidly on the warmed, dark parquet.

Ilya admired it out of the corner of his eye—the dog was very fine— but restrained himself and did not reach out to touch its incomparable fur. The Advocate might take such a movement for childishness, and Ilya had reason to fear that.

"Perhaps you've forgotten who I am?" he asked, shifting from foot to foot while the Advocate kept taking off and putting on his pince-nez, exclaiming greetings.

"Forgotten you, Gorbatov? You must think I've gone soft in the head! Sit down. I couldn't forget you no matter how hard I tried. The whole city is talking about you."

"About me?"

"Don't worry. You could not have come at a better time. You can speak at our public debate. People say that where you are in the South you've become something like a popular hero, as if you were already, to some extent, a mythological being."

Ilya clenched his teeth as hard as he could and actually ground them.

"Is that jarring? But my God, what a child you still are!" the Advocate went on, perching crosswise on the sofa in an extremely uncomfortable pose (he liked discomfort in moderation). "All Russian Paris is talking about you—and this must be taken advantage of. There's a rumor that you're not only taking trouble over the unemployed (speaking between us, you're going into competition with the Land Commission), they say you're removing an entire building here in Paris and you've fished a party of people out of Bulgaria! You've become quite the celebrity since the last time I saw you."

"No, all that, really, isn't quite right."

"Well, don't be angry at me, it's all because of your youth. Better you give an interview to *New Thoughts*. I'm on my way to their offices right now, we can go together. They're going to look at you as if you were a living Knut Hamsun hero and treat you well for that alone."

"No, no, please don't bring these things up with me," an embarrassed Ilya exclaimed. "No public debates, no interviews. I'm afraid of newspapers and have no idea how to behave with the public. I've come to have a friendly talk with you, if you'll allow me, otherwise I'll leave if you're going to insist on frightening me."

He was perfectly sincere, and the Advocate couldn't help notice that.

"A friendly talk with you is a pure pleasure for me, Gorbatov, but I confess I don't understand. Are you being modest or just capricious? I'll bring you out in our public debate. We're extremely curious to know your attitude toward loss of nationality, that terribly important—indeed, one might say crucial—question. You know, of course, that lately the number of people who have entered into mixed marriages (and from this, bear in mind, it is one step to taking French citizenship), the number of these people has been rising steadily, albeit slowly. And now, according to our observations, we have something puzzling going on. In the cities, the percentage of naturalized Russians is much higher than among those who have settled on the land, although one would think that the connection with Russia had been completely broken for the latter. These people not only don't switch to French citizenship, but in making mixed marriages they remain Russians on the inside, understand? It turns out that among those who are settling on the land, mixed marriages not only do not lead to loss of nationality, they also don't lead to a loss of the Russian principle in the families, whereas in the city . . ."

"Where are you getting this?" Ilya asked with a pounding heart.

"This is the result of our commission's research. A rather unexpected result, isn't it?"

"Not for me," Ilya replied, taking a breath. "I always thought that was the case, but I wasn't able to say so. That has been my personal experience."

The Advocate observed him curiously.

"I was expecting you'd say that, I confess," he said slyly. "Just yesterday a friend of mine conveyed to me your thoughts on this question and was surprised at you."

"I beg to differ, though. Yesterday this wasn't entirely clear even to me, and I've scarcely spoken to anyone about it!"

"Scarcely! I congratulate you! However, your thoughts did get as far as Morocco. My old friend Alexei Ivanovich Shaibin, recently returned from Africa, spoke to me about them."

In that instant Ilya thought he had misheard, that he was having an aural hallucination. His breathing stopped in his chest, and his heart started pounding with heavy, suffocating blows. For good reason! Shaibin was going around town talking about him! Shaibin was mentioning him! Shaibin was repeating his words!

"I must tell you the truth. My friend is quite skeptical, but you can take pride in the fact that your ideals permeated him at a distance. True, he's slightly démodé, but if you look closely, I, too, am slightly démodé." The Newfoundland wiggled its ears and growled. "And both these very démodé men are now awaiting the new word from you, the new man. If you don't want to take part in a public debate, so be it! But at least reveal to me the secret of your attitude toward the question that so interests us all right now."

Again—clouds of smoke and a leg crossed high in trousers stretched out by his knee. It was time for Ilya to say something, but he could barely collect his thoughts.

"You know I have no ability at all to speak the way you do," he began, remembering Kellerman, who could think so deftly about a hundred things at once. "I'll simply tell you what has occurred to me these past few days. Forgive me. I'll explain. These past few days it has become clear that my sister Marianna, who has now turned sixteen—actually, that's beside the point—is marrying the son of the owner of Au Paradis-Chevalin, that is, a horsemeat butcher, that's the name of the shop, and he is, of course, a Frenchman."

"Au Paradis-Chevalin is a horsemeat shop?" the Advocate said, horrified.

"Yes, Au Paradis-Chevalin . . . So, seeing all this, I started thinking and came to the conclusion—only this sounds a little silly and even somehow not scientific at all, you shouldn't be surprised—that the sole instance when a mixed marriage does not lead to a Russian's loss of nationality is a mixed marriage between people who settle on the land. People are uniting from different cultures, different faiths, and different languages outside the conventional framework of the modern European city, with its power to subordinate any culture, any faith, and any language. This leaves people free with respect to nationality. Coming to this conclusion, all that remained to say was that if this is so, and if mixed marriages are an inevitability for too many of us abroad, then we have to settle as many people as possible on the land. There, you see how simple and brief it is."

"No, Gorbatov, I think you've discovered your own little America," the Advocate said slowly and uncertainly. "Simple and brief it may be, but it's convincing.

Wait, though. Why exactly is this so? What is the explanation?"

"Oh, explanations are the hardest part." Ilya smiled suddenly and finally reached toward the Newfoundland. "After all, we're talking exclusively about us Russians, and that means the explanation has to be sought in our Russian breed itself. What plays a part here, more than likely, is that the land is the element closest to us, we're always at home on the land. Yes, for Russians the sole salvation from loss of nationality is the land."

"Yes, yes, Shaibin told me nearly the same thing yesterday," the Advocate exclaimed, throwing his head back. "He told me, If we don't follow this character (it was he who called you a character), we'll perish, apparently. Notice he said 'apparently.' He likes that word."

"He told you that?" Ilya asked, still not believing.

"Yes, Gorbatov, and it's significant. I asked him, What about your nice white hands, Alyosha? That infuriated him . . . But enough about him."

Ilya was so worked up, he was starting to fear losing his grip on himself, his words, his movements. No, Shaibin was positively out of his mind!

For a while the Advocate pondered, again curled up on the sofa.

"That means for you the question of the 'foreign threat,'" he began again, "is exhausted by the question of settling on the land? That means in your opinion one should settle on the land not only in the interest of the so-called pocketbook but also so that Russians can remain Russians?"

"Yes."

"If I may, there is one more detail here. If everyone 'settles,' then who will return to Russia? After all, you naturally are among those who think we're returning, right?"

The Advocate hitched up his shoulders and squinted. Ilya smiled again.

"Yes, of course I am. But you're mistaken. Everyone will return, that's the only reason they're going to go settle. Do you really think in your own, abstract way, that once someone's settled there he's going to remain? Why can't a cabinetmaker who's opened a workshop and found his own market for his work or an apprenticeship—why according to you will he necessarily return while those on the land won't want to?"

"You're a hard man, Gorbatov, and it's simply marvelous how all this finds room inside you! If you don't want to speak at our public debate, then at least help us and take part in working out our theses. What would it cost you?"

"I'm leaving tomorrow."

"Tomorrow! No, that's impossible."

"I can't otherwise. I have a family matter, that is, not entirely family and maybe not family at all. My brother is returning to Russia and I have to try to stop him."

"So you think this is a public matter?"

"Don't laugh at me, and trust me—that's almost the case," Ilya said, catching the Advocate's smile under his mustache. "He's something like bait . . . He's the focus of an entire organization that is catching people here and returning them to Russia."

"You know this for a fact?" the Advocate asked animatedly.

"Yes, but only since yesterday morning."

"Who from? Not Rastoropenko?" Ilya went on his guard.

"No, Rastoropenko didn't say anything to me. I saw him this morning. Admittedly, he and I had little to say, I was there under very strange circumstances."

"You do know, though, that he comes to see me?"

"I guessed as much. He could have met you at the Land Commission, and besides, he's the only person in Paris who knows about my involvement with the Bulgarian resettlers."

"So Rastoropenko didn't say anything to you?" the Advocate asked, clearly not wishing to end their intriguing conversation.

"No. Does he know anything?"

"He's had occasion to deal with a certain person. Oh, that occasion cost him dearly! Imagine, three months ago, Rastoropenko picked up a little Russian girl, an orphan, in some slum. He warmed her and fed her, but they themselves have nothing, and they had to give her away somewhere in the South, I can't tell you precisely where exactly, I only know they saved the little girl. Imagine, after a while a young woman of completely unambiguous appearance shows up and says she's the girl's aunt and demands her niece for herself. So he has to choose—the girl's twelve, and in two years her aunt's going to put her out on the street. We know these aunts! They went to all kinds of trouble and caused quite a scandal trying to persuade her to leave the girl in the South. But the woman would not stand down. She went to see them and said she was leaving for Russia soon and she was taking the girl with her. Basically, Rastoropenko drove her out. People say she's connected to a certain organization and she's on their payroll."

"As far as I know," Ilya said, firmly gripping the arms of his chair, "at the head of that organization is someone who arrived here about a week ago."

"You think?"

"Yes, I don't just think, I went to see him yesterday."

The Advocate took a jump on the sofa springs.

"What? You've already been there too!" he shouted, so that this time the Newfoundland shuddered and its ears went up. "There's no keeping up with you or surprising you. You're full of sensations you keep just to yourself. What did this new arrival tell you? Who is he?"

No, Ilya stubbornly decided not to reveal anything about Kellerman. This occurred to him the instant he gripped the arms of the chair, or a little bit before— now he couldn't remember exactly when.

"I'll surprise you again," he said, restraining himself. "I know the woman who went to see Rastoropenko. But I can't tell you anything more about the person who arrived from Moscow."

He said this and fell silent, and neither the Advocate's restless hands nor the Newfoundland could distract him this time. With those last words he decisively pushed away everything that was around him, this quite comfortable, vaguely ascetic room, with its fireplace, bed, and books, superb books more than likely, which stood on guard around the Advocate, cordoning off him and his thoughts and words.

He himself had pushed way back, and Ilya suddenly had no room for him in his thoughts.

"I give up!" the Advocate exclaimed with a brief laugh. "But the more I look at you, the more I'm confirmed in my previous opinion. Whether you like it or not, you are the hero of an unwritten novel that is certain to be written one day. In some future book you will occupy the place of honor of the 'positive hero,' but that won't happen soon, it won't until everything has settled down. But wait, when will everything finally settle down?"

"I found you so intriguing last summer," Ilya said, embarrassed, "and I'm so pleased to see you again. Only you're wrong. I'm not the hero of a novel and no one is going to write a book about me. I argue too little for a hero and act too simply, primitively even. Take Shaibin, your friend, he's a hero, probably, because he's connected to a constant, imperishable Russia, while I—how can I put it best?—I'm connected to a provisional Russia and for that reason I'm incidental to it. I was created by a catastrophic imperative, and if there are a lot like me, we'll accomplish something, but we aren't organic to Russia, we're loading the ship and taking away the gangways; others are sailing. My sister and brother are sailing, and you're sailing, and Shaibin, your friend, too, and it's his sailing that's the most important in our day. The people leaving at the end of this week to join us, join us there, they're sailing too, and that woman you were just talking about is sailing, oh, how she's sailing. We're just putting up the gangways and taking them away."

"But you've put something in motion now, and you're materially and morally safeguarding someone from perishing. Yes, you are actually pulling someone out of the swamp by the ears. People like you may be our best people. What gangways! That's all wrong. You're the captain, and if only you wanted it, our theoreticians would come listen to you. Even I—"

"None of that is possible," Ilya said, standing up, "because I don't live like the heroes in novels, because I have no ambition, not a drop of what is in many instances a sacred feeling, and there is no captain without that. There is in this world my stepmother. Someday I'll tell you about her. She wouldn't make a good heroine of a novel either; she, too, puts up gangways and takes them away when necessary. By the way, she wants to start a traveling school in the South."

The Advocate stood up too. It was quite clear that he would have nothing against Ilya staying another day, even two, for more conversations like this.

"Why are you in such a hurry to leave?"

"I have to move manure."

They were both silent for a minute.

"Please, Gorbatov, tell me," the Advocate said suddenly. "Who is that holy fool walking around there? People I know told me he stopped by to see them in D. They say he goes around, this old man, nearly blind, making up songs and singing them. What's this about?"

Ilya's face became almost harsh.

"I don't know, I haven't heard anything," he said. "I haven't seen any holy fools. I doubt they told you correctly."

"It's odd you don't know. We have a young writer here who was even going to go and write down the songs. You'll admit it's a fairly curious art, eh? Folk art two thousand kilometers from Russia, right?"

Ilya was quiet for a moment. It was time for him to go. And it was time for the Advocate, once left alone, to record something of this conversation in his note-book. There, in tiny, excruciating handwriting, a page had already been started, headed "On the debate over the emigration's fates."

CHAPTER SIX

A LEXEI IVANOVICH SHAIBIN showed up at the hotel on Sunday evening around eight. No one asked where he'd spent the night. He had a stale, aged look. One glance at him and it was clear the man was running out of money. No mistake about it.

He went to his room, where his bed lay untouched from the previous day, where everything had a very unlived-in look, and lit his pipe. It was clear from everything how terribly he'd agonized over the last twenty-four hours, and yet he was calm, a little pompous even, so that from that aspect, and especially thanks to his five-o'clock shadow, it might seem that here sat a gentlemen of forty-five or so, maybe even more, contemplating not trivial but at the same time not overly lofty matters.

The ceiling light was on, rain ran quietly down the windows, the street wept. At that evening hour (Ilya knocked on Alexei Ivanovich's door at about ten) all was decided for Shaibin, as he later admitted to Vera Kirillovna, although, of course, the decision he took at that time and which became the pivotal moment in our tale had been simmering inside him since somewhat before and was consciously clarified (with all its ramifications) only three days later.

It had been simmering—and this was impossible to conceal now—in Africa itself, when the name Ilya Gorbatov had been the most agonizing riddle, when Vera Kirillovna's letters, revealing to him for the first time the hardships of the Gorbatov path, had prepared him for a harsh and serious life. It had been simmering the past two nights as well—the first on the train (more unconsciously) and the second in the small, clean, and quiet brothel where he had gone perfectly sober just before nightfall (straight from his political friend's apartment) and where he drank a lot of cheap, strong wine and lay for several long, desolate hours alongside a taciturn and beautiful young woman.

For the first time in his life, this decision concerned his, Shaibin's, personal fate. Wasn't it time for him, a man who had grown up in "official comfort" and had found a second life in his recent "disappearance," to pass stern and unforgiving judgement on himself? Hadn't this second life been denigrated innumerable times in these past three days? Hadn't all his arguments been smashed by Ilya Gorbatov's mere existence and Vera Kirillovna's gentle but insistent words?

With a certain condescension toward himself, he recalled his visit to his political friend yesterday. They had never been friends, really; they were distant, very distant relatives, but out of the delicacy characteristic of civilized people they had never attempted to calculate this relation. The year this political friend had first gone abroad under gendarme escort was the year Shaibin graduated from high school. At the time, his own fate seemed much more enticing.

He recalled the previous day and his words about Ilya, pronounced loftily for the sole purpose of hearing them again from his own lips. Politically, his friend still had doubts about Gorbatov's ultimate correctness, and Shaibin tried to persuade him. It was rather odd to hear his own voice sounding confident, even a little crass. His political friend did not interrupt him. Then he himself began to speak. Reasoning that Shaibin had no reason to connive in his tendency toward abstractions, he immediately moved on to questions of mixed cropping, large grain farms outside Lyons, the Gascon three-field system, and the fact that sheep farming was faltering everywhere—but in vain!

Because Shaibin once again started shouting something about "Gorbatov's truth."

Only a full day later was he able to contemplate this whole impulse that had come over him after his wild flight from Nyusha's room and his walk through the cemetery. Now, as he sat in his hotel room, someone looking on might think this person was so calm, almost self-important, that he was about to pick up a piece of paper and a pencil, not an ordinary one but something special, and start calculating, scribbling something . . . He smoked his pipe.

In this hotel, where rooms were rented by the hour, or two, he heard constant steps, voices, and slamming doors. Outside, it was raining steadily, a fine rain, warm and long, and its drone accompanied an early, autumn night that advanced with the sky's blackness and the moving lights. The ends of the streets receded into a damp, crimson fog. The city began to quiet down. The cinema's piercing buzzer finished buzzing, automobiles stood in line at the corner waiting for the show to end. The hour's lull flew by. Then, suddenly, the doors of the nighttime restaurants started revolving; beggars stood on corners to whine at the evening passersby going from one lit doorway to the next, and young women gathered in threes and fours under café awnings. For the most part, they were all peasant girls, with large, still red hands, thick hair, and broad hips. Nothing could make them go back home, to the cows and chicken shit. They shouted obscenities, and men ran from them apprehensively.

It was around midnight, and above the Zanzibar, in the height of the black-green darkness, a bulging illuminated sign flashed, once every thirty seconds—attracting passersby and inflicting insomnia on the venereologist who lived on the first floor. Henri dashed between the little tables and the counter, where there was a wire stand with hard-boiled eggs and a barely touched, brick-red beef roast. He rushed back and forth with his mirrored tray and napkin—no, not spanking clean!

Lamps in seven colors drove the night into the sky, where over the roofs a blurred, rainy moon passed behind red clouds. A drunk got nabbed. Two women sat at a table and wept—Berta and Natasha—not that their names matter to us. Both were weeping over a letter. Henri asked them for the stamp because he didn't have a stamp like that; it depicted a sailor and the *Aurora*, but just go try to explain to Henri what the *Aurora* means. Never mind!

In Shpola, tiny, miserable Shpola, Berta's father, mother, Aunt Cecilia, sister Deborochka, and Grisha, the hope of the family, were once again being hounded over taxes. But their business hadn't been doing well for a whole year, the business in rubber soles and brass buttons had been important only for the comrade soldiers. Her father was in prison, his property seized. When was this going to end, Natasha? Or wasn't it, Natasha? They'd confiscated the money she'd sent them, Natasha. She felt so sorry for everyone—Papa and Deborochka and Grisha, the hope of the family. Do you know what Shpola is, Natasha?

Natasha wept very softly and kept blowing her nose, whether she needed to or not. What Shpola is? No, she didn't know. She'd never seen anything but Constantinople and Paris, and in Constantinople she'd been all of twelve. She barely remembered Russia. She'd also seen Biarritz, where she'd been taken and abandoned.

"Don't cry, Berta dear," she said through her tears, and she hid her face. "Look, those two gentlemen are laughing at us. Don't you cry and don't feel sorry for anyone. You have it harder than anyone, I always tell myself that you and I have it harder than anyone."

"But you're crying too," Berta whispered. "I can't bear it. Where will they go now? Where can they go? Mama scalded her hand with boiling water and can't sew, Aunt Cecilia is going blind and there's no money for an operation. Is this really not going to end before we reach the next world?"

She leaned her elbows on the table, pushed her black hat with the shiny buckle back even more, and turned up the fur collar of her dark coat. She had gentle white hands and a sweet, heavily made-up, Jewish face.

Natasha took out her compact. They sat silently, pressed close together, like two birds, training their inflamed eyes on an advertisement for Alsatian beer.

"You have it even harder," Berta said, summoning her strength. "Mine are far away at least, but yours are nearby."

"Shush!" Natasha fiddled with Berta's gloves and touched Berta's handbag—all things she'd seen a hundred times, familiar and dear, like her own, bought together, after long calculations and discussions, and at the sight of them she again felt like having a long, fervent cry.

"I went to see them today," Natasha said. "I got there, sat down by the door, and wanted to smoke—but I was afraid. My father was lying down, he'd cut out a portrait of Alexander III and hung it on the wall; he'll be at home until the first attack and then they'll take him back to the hospital, but the neighbors are complaining. My mother says, If you hadn't let that Englishman go, we'd be living somewhere in our own house now, outside Nice, for instance. She reproached me for my frivolous life. I left."

Berta closed her eyes.

"But what then, Natasha?" she asked very quietly.

"When then?"

"Then in general, in five years."

"The same thing, more than likely."

They pressed close together again. A lot of time passed. Someone next to them paid and left; others arrived.

"Know what?" Natasha spoke up. "Let's order an omelet."

Berta smiled with her tiny, even teeth and nodded. Yes, that was the best thing anyone could think to do. It would be nice to order some beer too.

Henri laid out a napkin, threw down forks, pepper, and bread with a ring and a clatter; beer like ice; an omelet sizzling in a skillet. The young women began eating the way they'd learned to here, in Paris, where life was harsh: so that not a crumb was wasted, so that everything they'd paid for went down their esophagus and into their blood.

"Maybe order a salad?" Berta asked.

They were served a salad and with it a cruet of oil and vinegar and mustard. Oh, what a consolation to dress the salad themselves! Only they had to be careful not a single leaf fell out of the cool white bowl.

The door opened wide. Shaking off her little umbrella, Merichka walked in, haughty and cheerful.

"Hello, Henri. What repulsive weather! Berta, you're here already? You're having supper? Why the long face?"

Oh, that Merichka. Nothing got past her!

She unbuttoned her fur coat to reveal her new dress, pistachio green, with a ruffle and silver—a fabulous dress! Stunning! She'd sung in it today, and look, the shoes matched so well, her old, last year's shoes, bought for seventy francs—there was a place like that.

Oh, that Merichka, she had no one, and how happy she was!

She twirled next to the table so that everyone started looking at her: the gentleman and lady, and the one who was alone, and those two men (neither of whom could be called a gentleman) sitting next to them who had long been silent and listening.

At last, Merichka sat down.

"Let's start dinner all over again," she said, and she rapped her agate ring on the table. To begin with, she ordered the dirty dishes cleared and paid for Berta and Natasha's beer, omelet, and salad. Then she spent a long time reading the greasy menu and choosing the most unusual dish.

"They took the piano out," said Berta, still talking

about herself, "that piano, Natasha." It had the one D with a crack, and when she played Liszt (wearing her black apron and braid), it distracted her. They'd removed the piano, and a hairdresser had cut off her braid.

The men stared at them, not taking their eyes off them. What provincials! Better not to look in their direction. Only from time to time would Natasha look up. For some reason she liked looking at the younger of the two; his jacket was separating at the shoulder seam. Was it too tight for him?

And then Nyusha Slyotova walked into the Zanzibar with her light step and sad, fixed face. She was wearing a rabbit fur coat—her only coat in the whole world. She surveyed the restaurant and saw everyone she needed to see.

"Henri," she said before she'd greeted anyone, "move these two tables together. Alyosha, meet Merichka, Berta, and Natasha. And you, Ilya . . ."

Entering right behind Nyusha was another three-some, also from the Palais des Boyards, one of them with a guitar. Then they moved a third table so every-one had somewhere to sit. Shaibin finally got up the nerve to say hello.

He himself would never have come here, of course, tonight, to these lights; it was Ilya who'd brought him.

Ilya said, "Nyusha made this date with me"—and so from the very start had provided the purpose and meaning of their entire evening together. At first they sat in Shaibin's room for rather a long time, almost talking, smoking and reading the evening paper. Then they went out in the downpour and ranged down the boulevard until they were soaked through. After midnight, they arrived at the Zanzibar, where for a long time they listened to the sobbing of the two young women and their Russian conversation. Ilya, a swollen vein in the middle of his forehead, sat perfectly still, distraught, staring at Natasha's face—which flustered her. Shaibin drank and the color gradually drained from his face, and the wrinkles that went from the wings of his slender nose to his chin began to look like two black laces. These conversations, these complaints, they were the same ones here three years ago. How could they change anyway? No one here could help anyone else.

Those who had come in after Nyusha, all three, were busy with the guitar, which one of them was holding at his stomach. This was a man once well known in Russia; his heavy nose and big oriental eyes adorned the covers of gypsy romances. Right now all that was left of this old sot's face were the thick eyebrows raised over the bridge of his nose in a particular tragic expression. His face was dark olive, his large jaw looked like the jaw of a dead horse, and what came out of his mouth wasn't a voice, it was a raspy whisper, sometimes high, sometimes low, depending on what the endless melody full of lyrical fermatas demanded.

The two who had arrived with him—one seriously drunk, wearing a Circassian coat and dirty, soft leather boots, the other wearing a dinner jacket, a dancer apparently, the kind who gets paid by the dance—both leaned toward him, their eyes half closed, and took in the minor progressions of certain gypsy variations with all the heartfelt lassitude of the night. With his large, sickly, very hairy fingers, the singer was strumming, stopping from time to time to make a foolish, surprised face, as if to say, Hey, that came out well! As if in his brilliant day he had never once happened to strum exactly that chord, had never once happened to move through this series of heart-wrenching sounds:

In a village, by a highway,
A gentleman loved a gypsy girl,
And his heart, abrim with worry,
Strummed the guitar's plaintive chord,

he repeated raspily for the tenth time, and his long face reflected his agitation over and over again, and tears were ready to spill from his cloudy eyes.

"Oh, you devil! Come on, one more time, Karpusha!" the man in the Circassian coat cried out, sniffing. "How finely it's put: strummed the guitar's plaintive chord! Not everyone can understand that, eh? Am I right, Lyosha? Not everyone can understand, a lout couldn't understand. It took dozens of generations with every bit of their aristocratic taste—smell, vision, and taste—for me to understand it!"

This speech drowned out Karpusha's voice, but he didn't try to fight the Circassian.

"I had a voice but I don't anymore, brothers." He drooped suddenly, and in the minute's silence they heard his deep, almost old-man sigh.

But no one sitting nearby paid the three any attention. The young women couldn't take their eyes off Ilya—all three fell hard for him right away. Nyusha opened her coat; she reeked of perfume.

"And this is Ilya Gorbatov," she said, pointing to Ilya. "He's got that ruddy face because he's always eating carrots. Not only that, he knows how to make people happy. Ilya, you should sell your recipes for 'what happiness is made of.' You'd make money."

Merichka laughed—and you couldn't tell whether she was sincerely cheerful or just pretending, she did it so well.

"You think we don't know how?" she exclaimed through her laughter. "Berta, we could sell our recipe too."

Berta was putting on lipstick.

"And this is Alexei Ivanovich Shaibin," Nyusha spoke again. "He doesn't know anything and doesn't want to know anything, and he couldn't care less about recipes."

Shaibin was sitting next to Ilya and like him didn't respond. He only quickly lowered his intense gaze so that no one could guess he'd been thinking about something else the entire time.

"Remember," he said, leaning toward Ilya very quietly, but as if there was no one else around, "remember I asked you on the train what you would do should I agree? You didn't answer."

Ilya turned slowly toward him, his face darkening.

"It's not for you to be dragging her away from here," he said, barely parting his lips. "Think of yourself. You couldn't possibly care what happens to her, otherwise you'd start coming here with a guitar."

Shaibin turned even paler, and the young women looked at him with annoyance.

"Why did you come back from Africa?" Berta asked. "Was it so bad there?"

Shaibin didn't hear the question, and Ilya answered for him.

"You mean you're from Africa too, seeing as how you know it's bad there?"

Nyusha knit her brow.

"Ilya, tell them where you've come from. Karpusha, listen! Lyosha!"

"I've come from the countryside," Ilya said cautiously.

"What countryside?" Natasha asked.

An impatient desire flashed across Nyusha's face for this conversation to finally come together. She was looking at Ilya almost imperiously and ignoring Alexei Ivanovich altogether.

"You mean you were in the country, staying at a dacha?" Karpusha asked, grinning pleasantly.

"No, I live there year-round."

"Poor health?"

"No, I work there."

Everyone fell silent again; Karpusha graciously said, "As do we here," and again picked up the guitar. But Nyusha made him be quiet.

"Who are you anyway?" Merichka asked.

"I'm a farmer." Ilya suddenly was embarrassed and blushed.

"What on earth is that?" Natasha again found the nerve to ask.

Now everyone's eyes were on him, and he didn't know what to do with himself. No, the conversation truly is not going to come together, Nyusha thought. You can't force Ilya to talk or you'll be done for with him. He doesn't know how to do anything. Look, he's put his fists between his knees and he's staring at the table. Maybe he's just unused to conversation, and now he's sitting like this as if he's lost all ability to think.

"I have a house there, oxen, leased land," he said at last, as if he'd squeezed out a massive weight. "A vegetable plot. Have you really not heard? Lots of Russians are living that way now."

"They wrote about it in the papers," Lyosha said.

"Yes, yes, that's it exactly, sometimes they do write about it there. So you see, well, I do it, and if you want to you can too."

Everyone fell silent.

"Do you have a piano?" Berta asked, her eyes open wide.

Shaibin suddenly raised his head. He seemed not to be hearing anything of what was going on around him, and he again leaned toward Ilya's ear.

"And what about my lameness? You've noticed I do limp a little. Will that get in the way?"

Ilya shuddered but wouldn't turn to look at Shaibin for anything in the world.

"No," he muttered brusquely, "it won't."

Nyusha was growing impatient; there was so little time left. She saw clearly now that Shaibin was preventing him talking and thinking. She couldn't contain herself.

"Please speak coherently, Ilya," she said uneasily, trying to meet his eyes. "That's why we came here," she lied, not blushing. "We're curious to hear about your life and your theories (he certainly does have theories!). Does really nothing come to mind?"

Shaibin woke up at the sound of her voice.

"It's an old Russian custom—talking in a tavern about life and Russia and all kinds of theories," he said, shuddering. "Don't tell me you're free of that curse, Ilya, after all, it's simply in bad taste now, by God!"

"And what if our entire life is the tavern and bad taste?" the man in the Circassian coat exclaimed in an injured voice. "What if we live and breathe the tavern?"

Lyosha immediately calmed him down without even glancing at Shaibin. Karpusha sat over his guitar, very drowsy.

"Forgive me, and quiet down, for God's sake," Shaibin said hastily. "Go on, Ilya, only what is this 'truth' of yours if it can both be offered up to these young Montmartre ladies and discussed in the League of Nations?"

Not surprisingly, no one paid Shaibin and his hard words any mind! No one except Berta, who suddenly blushed and bit her lip. But she didn't dare open her mouth.

Is he really jealous of me? The thought flashed through Ilya's mind, and he felt embarrassed.

"Alexei Ivanovich talks this way," he said, moving the objects on the table around, "because he's known all this for a long time and he's sick and tired of my conversation."

"What, you've talked to him about this?" Nyusha asked with alarm. "Did you perhaps suggest to him . . ."

"No, I didn't suggest anything to him."

Ilya felt Shaibin's light, hot hand on his arm.

"Not a word about me," Alexei Ivanovich whispered. To Ilya, that whisper seemed like the whisper of an accomplice, and he worried someone might have heard him, that on these grounds they might guess the turn in Shaibin's life that the Advocate had hinted at today.

"Fine, I'll tell you how we live there," Ilya began, in order to give Shaibin full cover. "I'll tell you, even though I know you're not at all as curious as Anna Martynovna says, and if you're not sleepy?"

Nyusha gave him a grateful look, the young women moved closer together, and Natasha put her hand on Berta's shoulder. Ilya ordered more beer.

"Wait a minute, let me go," Shaibin said suddenly. "There's no point in me listening to you. I'll go home to sleep. I actually stopped sleeping altogether the past few nights and even bought a powder at the pharmacy."

Alexei Ivanovich carefully extricated himself, and on his face was a peace such as Ilya had never seen before; without a smile, he bowed to everyone and to Nyusha separately. He started toward the door to general silence.

The thought that flashed through Ilya's mind at that moment was distinct, and its distinctness and timeliness was utterly unusual for him. Am I really able to think when I need to? he wondered. In an instant he had taken a pencil stub out of his pocket, torn an edge from the evening paper lying on the table, quickly jotted down a few words, and held them out to Alexei Ivanovich, who slowly took it and stuck it in the chest pocket of his jacket. But as Shaibin left the Zanzibar and went outside, where by that time the rain had ended and tires were swishing across the wet asphalt, he stopped.

Written on the newspaper edge was the address

of Mr. Rastoropenko. Shaibin read it twice. Alexei Ivanovich's fate was decided.

Meanwhile, Ilya was beginning his story. He barely looked at Nyusha and addressed himself to Merichka, then Berta, and even Natasha. Their gazes had again begun to follow him ecstatically. Karpusha and the man in the Circassian were drinking beer, in their drowsiness leaning their elbows on the table, and Lyosha was dunking sugar cubes in his brandy. Since at that late hour there were no other customers, Henri stood behind Merichka's chair, twiddling his fingers behind his back and hanging on Ilya's every word. He had the feeling that just as he was about to catch a few words—they would slip away, and he would chase after them.

Ilya was not telling his story quite the way Nyusha wanted. He said not a word about his thoughts, which he had spoken of so recently and so eagerly with the Advocate. He talked gaily and at length about Gabriel and Marianna, about how a fair had come to their town in the summer and they'd ridden a cow together, about how it all started for them with that; he talked about Saint-Didier, where people strolled sedately on holidays, about Monsieur Jolifleur and how, when he saw Marianna riding the cow behind his son, that same day, late that night,

Monsieur Jolifleur had come to the Gorbatovs' farm and peeked through the window—he wanted to know what kind of people these Russians were—and seen Marianna under the lamp, in her apron, beads around her neck and a ring on her finger, and taken a liking to her.

He talked about his former boss, a rich landowner and the mayor, the owner of the very forest that had stood there since year one and that was now undergoing unprecedented changes; about shares in the canning company—maybe some of you have even seen those slim green tins, they're sold in all the stores? That was the famous asparagus. He talked about the future grain, about the wheat, and finally about Vera Kirillovna, who in the first year saw her garlic and leeks die in the garden because of that cursed *Puccinia allii*, and how she'd wept then; how last year she'd had a new dress sewn for herself in town, by the seamstress, and how Marianna was getting ready to have a new one sewn for herself for the spring. He talked about the Russian farmhand who'd spent the summer with them and left for the Gascogne, to sharecrop, and about how he wanted to hire someone again for the spring, to train him and send him to a piece of land outside Toulouse. That was all. He told them what he knew.

"And your brother Vasya?" Nyusha asked impatiently.

Ilya had nothing to tell them about Vasya; for a minute, no one said anything. Even him.

"Life is hard," Merichka said suddenly, squinting. "It always seems as though it's so easy, but if you think about it—no, there's nothing easy about it! It's just hard. Maybe you'll tell us some more?"

The man in the Circassian coat struck the table with his hand, its nails curved like a vulture's.

"Let's go, Lyosha, eh? Don't you want to? Let's go dig potatoes! Karpusha, don't sink to the bottom, brother, rise up! We're going to go tug Mother Earth's teats!"

"Quiet, don't make a scene," Berta turned to them quickly. "Oh you men, you drunk men, incapable of anything! Our Grisha here would probably go, he'd probably get up the nerve, and he'd take all of us with him! Oh, what's the use of talking!"

"He won't take us," Nyusha whispered to her sadly. "Besides, we need so much else for life. Poor us. Right, Merichka?"

"Right, Nyusha." She nodded, and there were two tears in her eyes. "Only no. No! We don't need anything, we don't. We're happy as we are!"

All four young women understood each other at a glance.

"We're happy as we are!"

He felt he couldn't be present at this merrymaking any longer, but Karpusha wanted to sing a parting song. He asked them to listen. He strummed a few chord progressions for a long time, raising his caterpillar-like eyebrows higher and higher.

> In a village, by a highway,
> A gentleman loved a gypsy girl,
> And his heart, abrim with worry,
> Strummed the guitar's plaintive chord,

he declaimed hoarsely to the soul-stirring accompaniment, and suddenly began to weep.

"I can't sing, I can't breathe anymore, brothers," he said through his sobs.

"Let's go right now"—Natasha jumped up—"Otherwise he'll make us all cry, like yesterday."

The young women stood up. Now there was something similar in them all, something that drew them closer, and it was clear from just a fleeting glance that they'd lived together a long time and been through a lot together.

Ilya stood up too. Nyusha said, "You and I need to talk, Ilya. Let's take a short walk, all right? I have something to discuss with you."

The young women shook Ilya's hand silently. The other three stayed behind. There was less than an hour until Zanzibar closed, and they shut the place down every night.

The rain had stopped long before, so the street had had time to dry out. The clouds had parted to show a mild and distant pre-dawn sky. In a corner café where the door was wide open and cheap tobacco smoke came billowing out, Negroes wearing just vests but with watches on chains were playing billiards. Their teeth and the whites of their eyes flashed at Ilya like the whiteness of billiard balls. Nyusha took him by the arm and led him away. He didn't recognize the streets, paper and litter were carried on the wind, the streetlamps' sickly light spread over the sleepless faces of passersby, and pale illuminated advertisements shuddered and went out; with every minute the sky was getting more transparent and the stars high up were drowning in the light. In the window of a large restaurant, on a dissolute square with an empty fountain, a sweaty violinist was finishing up, and from the narrow, gilded door a richly and badly dressed woman with pearls worth a hundred thousand wrapped around her repulsive neck was descending the spit-covered steps to a rattling automobile.

At the corner of the boulevard, where it was deserted and quiet, Nyusha stopped and looked into Ilya's face.

"Do you know why I made a date with you at the Zanzibar?" she asked in anguish. "When have you decided to go home? This evening?"

"Yes, on the seven-twenty train."

She took him by the sleeve and came so close they were almost touching.

"Ilya, look. I'm begging you"—she could barely speak—"leave this morning, right now. I know there's a train at about eight. Listen to me, I'm begging you."

This was the last thing he'd expected (in a foolishness he wouldn't have admitted to himself for anything, he'd even imagined she was going to say she'd decided to go with him). But why did she need him to leave Paris twelve hours early?

"Haven't you already been everywhere you wanted to be?" she asked, affectionately raising her face to his and immediately lowering her eyes. "Do you really need Monday too? You must go, listen, you absolutely must. Leave this morning. It's just after five now; you have to be at the train station in three hours."

He didn't say anything, waiting for her to reveal the reason for her request herself, but the longer he was silent, the more agitated she became.

"You have to go. Why didn't you tell me anything about Vasya? You have to get there before it's too late. This evening Adolf sent him a telegram in your name, you're supposedly summoning him—"

Ilya tried to restrain himself in vain—he jerked his hand from Nyusha's. The faces and events of the past two days ran through his memory. He saw Adolf leaning over the railing and shouting after him purposely contrived words, he saw the Advocate's grimace when he told him about the woman who had gone to Rastoropenko's apartment; and Anyuta flashed before him as he'd seen her on the road, and the courtyard where the children were digging in the garbage.

For a minute he looked in silence at Nyusha's lowered head in its bright felt hat.

"Who are you?" he asked cruelly, as if seeing her for the first time. "Are you really in cahoots with Kellerman?"

She stood there, not moving.

"Did he really get you mixed up in his work? And you agreed! You went to see Rastoropenko to disgrace yourself! My God!"

"First tell me you'll leave right away, with the first train," she said stubbornly.

"Why do you care?"

She took his hand again; her head was spinning.

"This is the only thing I can do. There's no other way I can help. Quiet! You're prepared to think I'm in cahoots with Adolf, that I'm a fool they've conned, at best. No, that's not true. They tortured me. I've known Adolf since last year; he was keeping Merichka and dropped her. I latched on to him and all his promises—anything to escape this vulgar life. But he didn't need me; he needed the people he could get to through me. But I swear to you, I swear he won't learn Rastoropenko's address from me! Will you go?"

"Yes," Ilya said.

He took her arm and this time they walked very slowly. Where? Down the boulevard, where there was no one at this hour—just beggars sleeping on benches.

Nyusha was sending him away—this was clear to Ilya—she was consciously losing him, she was giving him up. She had betrayed Kellerman to him. Why? In an attempt to save Vasya?

"You say he sent a telegram in my name? You mean you want Vasya rescued? You want to be with us against Adolf?" he asked. This is wrong, wrong, flashed through his mind.

"I want at least someone to be rescued," she whispered, looking straight ahead.

"Have you known Adolf long?"

"As I said: about a year. He put Merichka up in a hotel, and I met him at her place."

"And while you were writing to me and waiting for me you were hoping your rescue might come from him?"

"I'll tell you, Ilya, I was prepared to go to Russia."

He squeezed her arm involuntarily.

"And now?"

"Now, no. Now I see what kind of people they are. After all, their entire correspondence with your brother happened right in front of me. He wanted me to write to you, to break you with my 'charms,' or something. Oh, he said, there's no one who can't be bought! Now I see what kind of man he is. And now it's all come to me at once: I'm betraying him and losing you forever."

She looked into his eyes with determination. She had surprised herself: she had no desire to complain of her fate or cry. Yes, she was utterly bereft, but hadn't it been he, Ilya, who had planted the wild belief in a miracle in her?

"Tell me, what would you want for yourself? Now that I'm deleting myself from your life, what would you want for your own happiness?"

He was pushing her toward thoughts she feared, thoughts she resisted. She turned red; her arm became light and weak in his.

"I told you," she said, as if still defending herself. "I need someone, it can't be any other way. I'll drop everything, I have nothing against hard and steady work, I'm even searching for that, but I can't alone, I need love. I thought you were that love, but you didn't return my love, and I see I'm so weak that I can't fight your indifference, your friendship. That means I'm saying goodbye to you in my heart. And I'll start searching all over again."

"You have to search not among firsts, not among those who can become firsts without you, you have to find the weakest, the real lasts. They'll recognize you there, they'll love you there ... I searched for those farthest away from me—in Bulgaria, here in Paris, in that building where Rastoropenko lives—you were there too, after all, which means you know what that is. Vera Kirillovna, you know, too, where she searched—in the Foreign Legion."

She glanced at him, and he guessed the question in her eyes.

"And found him," he said quietly.

His heart was full. It was as if he were drunk from the wine he'd had at the Zanzibar. He should be ashamed, really! A country boy came to Paris and drank too much and was prowling the streets until dawn! No, clearly life in the countryside imposed unavoidable rules on a person.

They turned through the streets, now gray in the dawn. Burly milkmen raced by, garbage pails were carried out of buildings, and an enormous truck, panting, went from one corner to the next collecting them. There, his legs spread wide and his sleeves rolled up, a young fellow was dumping the contents of those zinc pails at his feet, and from time to time his merry gaze would fall on a kitten's crushed little body, or a worm-eaten ficus pot. And with a soft, bedewed rustle another truck passed by, wide-backed like the first, and poured water on the square, dousing the street air with freshness; and that fellow, maybe the brother of the one hovering over the garbage, just as cheerfully and proudly shifted gears, turned the taps, and leaned against the wheel with his whole body.

Not another word was spoken between Ilya and Nyusha. He said goodbye to her on the staircase landing. She told him to tell Marianna that she remembered her and wished her happiness in her marriage (he never did buy the lilac soap!).

She ran upstairs and stood on the landing for a minute, listening for Ilya to go into his room. Then she quickly went into her own, undressed in the darkness (the blinds were drawn), washed, picked up a pillow, her own, in its lacy cover, locked the door, and went to the end of the hallway, to Merichka's. Very quietly, she slipped in with her under the blanket, and Merichka, waking briefly, mumbled something incoherent and affectionate and put her arms around her. They fell asleep pressed close together, so that in the morning Nyusha Slyotova was not in her room and it took a while for them to find her.

But Ilya was afraid to go to bed, afraid of falling sound asleep for fourteen hours. His heart was full of alarm and joy. He neatly packed his few things and carried them downstairs. It was quiet there. He went outside and had coffee and a roll in a coffeehouse that had just opened, where the owner himself was sweeping yesterday's litter from under the counters. Ilya sat there until six o'clock and read the morning paper.

Indeed, he did not have anything more to do in Paris, he was free to leave in the morning instead of the evening, but the evening train was an express and the transfer more convenient. If he left Paris in the morning, he wouldn't be home before ten o'clock that evening, and he would have to go on foot from the station through the nighttime fields, under the moon, alone—how wonderful that would be!

At seven o'clock he returned to the hotel, paid his bill, and left for the station, where he patiently waited nearly an entire hour for them to pull in the train. There were a lot of people. It seemed to him that the same woman was traveling next door, in the next compartment, as had traveled to Paris with him three days before, and the same Arab was standing by the window. The quiet streets and gardens of Maisons-Alfort passed quietly, the Seine flashed a leaden gleam, barques, swans. Ilya stretched out on the hard berth and fell asleep, fist under cheek, to the unforgotten, even murmur of the wheels.

He got up about three times on the whole journey, no more, bought food and beer at the stations and then lay down again. There wasn't anyone on the facing bench. The wheels knocked, the train raced from north to south, the day was damp and gloomy, smoke burst through the train car window, and low, smoky clouds waved their sleeves at Ilya.

He woke up in A., greeted by a soft southerly wind and a quiet evening. The train rushed on, toward summer, toward the sea, where people were still bathing, toward shores in flowers and white stone.

He was on home territory again, he was again close to that piece of land, that place in the world he hoped to belong to from now on. What did the city and the forty-eight hours he'd spent there mean to him? They had dissolved behind his back in the early twilight of the northern autumn, leaving behind only a memory—a memory of human frustration and futility. Ilya wasn't thinking about himself. While the small, loud train was taking him home, what passed through his thoughts, slowly, somewhat irrevocably, but with a calm distinctness, were Nyusha and Shaibin, until at last he started thinking only of Vasya, whom he should see in an hour and with whom he faced a major and open fraternal struggle.

The train stopped for half a minute, and Ilya hopped off. Outside it was night and smelled of damp leaves. "It must have just rained," Ilya thought, and his heart started pounding with joy. He walked down the platform, past the attendant, and into the small, lonely station. Two lights burned over the ticket window and the door creaked repulsively. There was no one anywhere around.

The town was sleeping a solid, amiable sleep. Shutters were closed; only in the corner bakery, in the basement, there was a light, which looked red from far away. On the main street, washed by the rain, the rare streetlamp was lit, and Monsieur Gastonet's establishment was still open. Across the way, catching its cheerful lights, Monsieur Jolifleur's sign flickered. It was quiet, sleepy, and fresh, like in his room at night when the window was open. Ilya carried his suitcase through the still town; at its edge, the trees were whispering to each other. Suddenly, turning left, he saw a familiar expanse; somewhere, as if right on the horizon, a dog was baying. Before he had gone twenty steps, a barely nibbled moon rose behind a distant black hill, rose with a magical swiftness and hung over the distant forest, and everything sprang to life in its cool light. The sky and its suddenly diminished stars receded high and away, the land felt close all the way to the horizon, and Ilya's shadow fell far to the right, toward the last houses on the outskirts of town, toward the school's vegetable garden, and there crept away.

He walked and walked, and the farther he got from town, the more insanely and fervently he loved this night and this land, the familiar clump of trees by the road, the silence in the air, the deep silence of the tidy fields. He felt no shame—he was ready to start singing. Hat in hand, he walked fairly quickly, his lips catching the wonderful breath coming toward him. Yes, there was no doubt, today it had rained a little: the road was darker, the stars were washed clean . . . Lord, I thank You!

It was here, at this turn, that he and Shaibin had boarded the bus three days before, and just about now he would see the tall plane trees and the roof of his house, and the attic where Vasya probably was, asleep or not, most likely not, agonizing. Yes, the plane trees and the house behind them were unshakably firm; Ilya saw them in the night's quiet and light.

At that point he could no longer resist the happy flutter that came over him. Then and there, on the damp road, he got down on his knees and pressed his chest to the clayey, friable soil. And in the ensuing silence (before, he hadn't been able to hear anything but his own steps) he could make out the night's crackles and rustles in the grass by the road.

He cautiously unlocked the gate, and the dog ran up to him and with a quiet rumbling pressed up to his knees. Evidently they'd long been asleep in the house, and for some reason the kitchen window was hung with Marianna's apron. Ilya walked toward the outside stairs leading to the attic; the dog kept getting underfoot.

Cautiously, he began ascending; he didn't want to awaken Vasya or those sleeping downstairs. Cautiously, he opened the attic door and in the gloom saw the familiar outline of the two beds: on one of them, bundled up in the darkness, someone sat looking silently in his direction, as if long awaiting him.

"Vasya," Ilya said quietly, stopping at the threshold.

"He's not here," Vera Kirillovna replied, getting up. "He's gone, Ilyusha. He left us yesterday evening."

He couldn't see her pallor, but her eyes glittered with tears. Ilya perched on the stool by the door. In one instant the happy flutter flew from his soul.

"I was waiting for you. I had a feeling you'd come," Vera Kirillovna said, approaching him. "Saturday evening I realized it was all over, he wasn't going to wait for you. I even thought he was in a hurry and wanted to catch you in Paris. Something strange began to happen with him. In the morning, on Sunday, he spent a long time with the animals, and then in town; Gabriel admitted he'd come to him for money and said Gabriel could have his, Vasya's, pay in the morning and you hadn't left any money. Meanwhile, Jolifleur was here and Marianna is betrothed. In the evening, after supper, Vasya left. He didn't come back yesterday or today—he's gone."

"He swore he'd say goodbye to me," Ilya said.

The two found themselves a step apart, in total darkness. Ilya reached out and found Vera Kirillovna's trembling hand. Several minutes passed.

"Mama, you and I have always sought out the hardest paths," Ilya said muffledly, "paths that are too much for others. It was too much for Vasya, but someone else will come to take Vasya's place, and maybe more than one, and maybe one day even Vasya will return."

She started trembling even harder.

"Tell me, Ilyusha, don't shut me out," she whispered. "What's going on with you? Tell me . . ."

"No, no, there's nothing I can say, I myself have no idea."

She pulled her hand back and covered her face.

"When will the money be sent?" Ilya asked. "The people are ready, they could leave on Friday."

"Jolifleur got the money today and said he'd send it to Rastoropenko tomorrow."

She walked past him like a shadow. He followed her, his soul bursting from pity.

"Do you know who's downstairs?" she asked timidly, holding the door jamb. "He's in the kitchen, spending the night here with Anyuta. They brought him from L. after dinner. In three days they'd covered twenty-five kilometers, that's all. He'd started feeling unwell and gave them our address. The little girl is frightened. He's very weak."

Ilya heard her whisper. Now he held the ends of her scarf.

"Do you know who this little girl is? He didn't tell you?"

"No, he hasn't said anything at all. He's coughing a lot. He has a fever."

"Tomorrow at break of day send Marianna for a doctor."

"He doesn't want a doctor."

Her whisper and the rustle of her movements dissolved somewhere very close to Ilya. She ran her hand lightly over his head and went out. He listened to the outside steps creak.

And so, somewhere around Dijon, his train had crossed paths with Vasya's. His locomotive had flown toward him with a deafening whistle, the cars had rattled, the two noises merging into one, and other windows, train car walls, intermittent openings had flashed in the windows. He'd seen none of this, known none of this. And now it was all over with Vasya. His long journey had at last been decided.

CHAPTER SEVEN

"HELLO THERE, MUZHIK," Adolf said archly.

"Hello," Vasya said.

The people rushing off the train wouldn't let them stop, bustled them off to the exit.

"Where are your things?"

"I don't have any."

He wasn't even wearing a coat, and it was clear he had shivered all night on the train: his nose was red, and his hands, which stuck out of his jacket sleeves, were even slightly purple. He had a disheveled look.

"You see," Adolf began, now quite condescendingly, "I have to admit that the telegram sent to you Saturday afternoon was from me. Ilya could not have sent you a telegram, of course."

"I realized that." Vasya nodded. "Ilya wouldn't have."

"Is that so? That means you've decided to go? All the better."

"I've decided, but I gave Ilya my word I wouldn't leave without saying goodbye to him. That's why I was in such a hurry, so I'd catch him here and we wouldn't miss each other."

Adolf frowned.

"Well, you misjudged, muzhik. He left this morning. They told him you'd been summoned and he rushed off to grab you by the tail."

Vasya stopped. His red cheeks now seemed puffy, and his frightened, faded eyes aroused sympathy in the passersby.

"I'm not going to see him?" he mumbled. "But I swore to him . . ."

"This isn't your fault, it's his, for not waiting for you."

They got into an automobile.

"Fourteen, rue Ganneron," Adolf said. "I'll take you to your hotel and you'll leave tomorrow."

Vasya looked at Adolf thunderstruck, not recognizing him at all. Not only that, he was very hungry.

"How do you know Ilya left?" he managed to ask.

His questions irritated Adolf.

"He was told yesterday the telegram had been sent, and given what he's like, he couldn't sit here, could he? I also just called the hotel."

"He was told on purpose?" Vasya asked helplessly.

"That's none of your business. My God, Vasya, what a bumpkin you've turned into!"

That's what he calls my automatic reactions, Vasya thought. Suddenly he felt guilty. Here he was in Paris, here he was on a journey he himself had chosen. No, he was simply no use for anything!

They sped down the broad, busy boulevards.

"Is that the Arc de Triomphe?" Vasya asked.

"No, that's the Porte Saint-Denis."

There was absolutely nothing to talk about with him.

"Don't think I'm a complete fool," Vasya said, "it's just that I don't feel like conversation."

"Are you upset, doubting yourself? I understand. You're the same young lout you were before."

It doesn't matter, better not to respond, Vasya thought. Where are we going? I wish we'd gone straight from one train station to the other.

But from Adolf's rude, disjointed words it became clear that Vasya's train was leaving tomorrow evening, at 7:10. Until then, he was free. He could go to the movies this evening, *Street Angel* was playing. "You probably haven't been to the movies in three years, have you? Not only that, you can buy yourself a coat. I'll give you some money. No, you can't go see Alexander Adolfovich. He's too busy."

The gasoline and dust revolted him with their trace sweetness. At the hotel, Adolf himself reached an agreement with the concierge. Yes, of course, we have a free room, the same one the man from Provence freed up early this morning.

"I'm leaving you five hundred francs. Buy a coat and get by until tomorrow. I'll come for you at about six o'clock and bring you your ticket and passport."

Vasya stood in the middle of the room holding five hundred-franc bills. How simple it all was, how incredibly simple! Something like this could only happen to him because he was insignificant and pathetic, because life was speeding by.

Adolf left, and now Vasya knew what he had to do. This one thing had tormented him the whole night. He calmly looked at the money, stuck it in his pocket, ran downstairs, and asked where the post office was.

He got lost twice in the noisy, brightly lit streets. Finally, after standing in line for a long time—at the end of the month there are always a great many money transfers—he sent Gabriel the two hundred francs he'd borrowed the day before. After he left the post office, he bought two pairs of sausages and a pound of hot cabbage in a butcher shop and ate all that in his room, having forgotten about bread.

He had to survive this way for nearly two whole days. He didn't know anyone in Paris and could not even contemplate sleep. Outside it was cheerful and fresh, but he didn't have a coat or the money to buy one; Vasya didn't know exactly what a Paris coat might cost. He sat by the window and began watching the street. He despised himself, he was disgusted by everything that had anything to do with him. He saw himself as hypocritical, foolish, and unworthy of anyone's love, having betrayed Ilya and deceived Vera Kirillovna. He was especially ashamed, almost horrified, to think of Marianna, her broad laborer's back when she mixed the slop for the hogs, her eyes, her happy, lovesick eyes when she looked at Gabriel. Everything not directly related to him—as if he were infected with a bad disease and spreading a silent infection—everything had an inexplicable and sweetly humiliating charm for him.

He thought of Terenty Fedotov, the farmhand who'd worked for them this summer. Fedotov had never quite understood that they could have gotten along perfectly well without him. Ilya had purposely hired him in order to teach him, to give him the opportunity to set himself up independently by the autumn. Fedotov had gathered three countrymen (one even brought his wife) and settled about three hundred kilometers away. Ilya had even explained his contract to him.

No, no, he couldn't live there or here. This is the kind of hotel where people usually go to shoot themselves, he thought. He wasn't going to shoot himself, he was going to try out one more way of life. Most likely his dear papa, Stepan Vasilievich, would meet him at the Moscow station, the same one they'd all departed from once upon a time; and then this poison would already be inside him, but it would be secret. Adolf had surfaced from the underground with all his letters; Adolf had let this poison pour through his veins.

The first letter had come a year before. Yes, a year exactly. At the time, Adolf had only asked him, Do you want to? And Vasya had answered, I do, I do, but I don't believe it. Many months passed after that, and at one point in the spring he'd stopped answering Adolf altogether; that was at Easter, after that man, that blind old man, that former country teacher, people said, had spent time at their farm.

He no longer remembered a single word of what that unusual guest had said. He couldn't remember a single one of his songs. Now, when the wayfarer had come back to see them at the farm, enfeebled and completely blind, there was as before no kindness, no forgiveness in him. What kind of Christian was it who was full of such sternness, such strictness? He blessed those close to him, but sent an anathema against those far away, asked God to bring them disease and hunger. Vasya didn't get to know their new visitor well, and that would torment him in Moscow. And Ilya? For three years he'd watched him plow, thresh wheat, build a shed, chop down the crooked tree by the road that had for a long time, thirty years probably, been a hindrance to the postman and everyone else. For three years he'd walked behind him "without understanding anything," as Vera Kirillovna said. "You'll come back when you do." Empty words. Impossible! Come back? How? Why? I can't come back in an everyday, heart-felt way. No, anyone who ends up there doesn't come back. But who does end up there?

"Self-seekers" (Marianna's word) looking for an "easy life." Am I really one of those? Vasya thought. Do I really want to be idle and . . . a scoundrel? I want a homeland, that's what I told Ilya. Above all, a home-land should resolve the fundamental questions of my existence—and that's a relief in itself. Here I don't hear its voice. Yes, I want relief, I want to be there so I don't feel responsibility for the main thing and I'm not master of my own life. Here I'm too free.

He raised his head; he thought he'd heard a knock

at the door. But there was no one to knock so he didn't respond.

I have too much freedom, more than I'm ready for, he told himself with a precocious sorrow, and once again glanced at the door. The knob turned slowly and the door opened a crack.

"Ilya, are you asleep?" someone's voice asked.

Vasya jumped up.

"Ilya? Ilya's not here," he exclaimed in fright.

The door suddenly flung open, and Vasya saw Shaibin.

For a minute they stood facing each other, as if they were strangers. They stood silently, not taking their eyes off each other, stunned by this meeting.

"Vasya Gorbatov?" Alexei Ivanovich asked, slowly catching his breath.

He walked in, and right then Vasya noticed for the first time that his left leg was slightly lame. Not only that, he noticed that this man, who had spent a whole day with them, had changed markedly here, in Paris. Even then he'd had a far from brilliant look, but now his eyes were inflamed and his whole face had a gray cast.

"You've come to see Ilya?" he asked, evidently embarrassed at his own curiosity. "Ilya left this morning."

Shaibin understood nothing from these words.

"Left for where?" he asked patiently.

"Home," Vasya replied.

At that moment, Alexei Ivanovich realized he'd been left on his own, and simultaneously with this thought another occurred: Ilya was gone, leaving him different from how he'd been when he brought him here, Ilya had left him when he wasn't afraid anymore, Ilya had run off after accomplishing what he was supposed to do, what Vera Kirillovna had sent him to do.

"Why are you here?" Shaibin asked, vaguely recalling something. All these days he'd been so caught up thinking about himself that he'd completely forgotten about Vasya for a while. "What are you doing here, in Paris, in this hotel?"

"I'm staying here. I missed Ilya. I'm leaving tomorrow."

Ah, yes! Little Vasya, a grown man now, was leaving for Russia. Shaibin had heard this in the South. But was it really true?

"So you want to be lost?" Alexei Ivanovich asked involuntarily.

Vasya looked at his feet.

"Is this you, Alexei Ivanovich? I'm hearing this from you?" He'd summoned his nerve.

Shaibin closed the door.

"I'm only asking, I'm not telling you what to do, although . . . I could. You ran away from home?"

Vasya didn't answer.

"Fine, I don't need an answer, you've already given your answer. Look at yourself in the mirror: you look like a thief. You deceived Vera Kirillovna."

Vasya turned red and tried hard to hide it.

"What about you?" He grinned and was frightened at his own words.

Shaibin stood there calmly between door and sink. Never in his life had he had occasion to hear such words. His entire life, his entire self, with his ambivalent thoughts, his ailing heart, which got him an early discharge from the Foreign Legion, everything that surrounded him—including Nyusha, who had tormented him briefly and meanly—everything suddenly came crashing down, lost beyond recall, beyond rescue, in some abyss. All that remained was his guilt, the guilt of his whole life.

He did not look away under Vasya's gaze. Vasya was sitting by the table, red and disheveled.

"Your question is timely," Alexei Ivanovich said bitterly, "but my life isn't over yet, even if I do look like an old man to you. Do you know how old I am? Forty-two. Oh, if I were your age, everything would be different, believe me. I wouldn't be talking to you right now. I'd be rushing upstairs like mad to find out whether she went with him—but, as you see, I'm not rushing anywhere, I'm listening to you, and answering you, and at this very moment, in my heart, I'm even making up my mind about an action of tremendous importance, tremendous significance for myself. Only now (and quite slowly, you'll note) am I going there. Maybe this makes me an old man? No, this means something completely different . . ."

He truly did open the door unhurriedly and walk toward the stairs.

Vasya stood up, and understanding very little, hesitating, followed him.

He couldn't stay behind. He followed Alexei Ivanovich up the stairs, and his curiosity was so intense that, when he reached the top landing, he even asked himself: Where was Shaibin going and what did all this mean? Shaibin didn't look back. Reaching Nyusha's door, he stopped and knocked. He knew he was doing this out of some cruel necessity; he felt no unease. No one answered his knock. There was no key in the lock. Maybe deep down he wished she'd stayed after all, that she hadn't left with Ilya? No, he did not have that wish. Nyusha didn't belong to him anymore; it was all over with her. "You're not curious about me"—after words like that people can never be intimate again.

He knocked again. Clearly she'd gone. That meant Ilya loved her, if he took her away, that meant everything had ended as it should. That meant he'd kept her for himself and not given her to Alexei Ivanovich, like the most ordinary, the most common rival. No, impossible! He hadn't taken her away ... Perhaps she'd gone after him? Meekly latched on to him? Poor Nyusha!

He rattled the door. No one. Nothing. It would have been better if she'd stayed on, after all. How was she going to work in a field? Was she Marianna, to work in a field? She should stay here—someone would turn up for her here. And let Vera Kirillovna reign alone there, at least there would be none of this perpetual unease, this unfaithfulness, this captivity. With Vera Kirillovna. Alongside Vera Kirillovna.

Shaibin stood there so deep in thought that this time Vasya thought he might be unwell. Then for the first time he saw that quick, terrible spasm that contorted Shaibin's face, which up until then Shaibin had so assiduously concealed from him, as he had from the others. Vasya thought Alexei Ivanovich might be unwell, that he might need help, but he didn't know how to console people, especially forty-year-old men with a mysterious past—and for Vasya, Alexei Ivanovich's past was definitely mysterious. Do people take them by the arm and lead them away somewhere, or bring them water, or, just the opposite, pretend they don't notice their condition?

Minutes passed, and Shaibin was still standing at the door. The hotel was quiet, it wasn't a time for making noise, the people who stayed here went to bed late, and by morning the alcohol had made their sleep especially sound. Vasya was still standing alongside Alexei Ivanovich. He asked, not for the first time, most likely:

"Who's staying here?"

Again Shaibin didn't answer, but Natasha's tousled head poked out of the door across the way. Glancing at the two standing in the hallway only briefly, so she could immediately lower her sleepy eyes, Natasha covered her puffy face with her hand, yawned, and said, "What's all the racket, like you owned the place! She might be with Merichka, in forty-one." And she immediately closed the door.

And Alexei Ivanovich didn't look around; he quickly proceeded down the hallway.

When Nyusha appeared in the doorway wearing Merichka's robe, which was too long for her, her face startled and pink from sleep, Shaibin felt as though Ilya loomed too large in his life. Nyusha was here, she hadn't left with him. No, Ilya had not deceived him while Shaibin slept after taking his powders!

He took her by the hand, which at first she really didn't want to give him, and led her almost forcibly out of the room into the hallway.

"So you didn't leave with him?" he asked, and there was a malicious glee about Ilya's freedom in his words. "He didn't take you and leave?"

"I know he's gone," she said, timidly. "Leave me alone. You've lost your mind."

"I'll leave you, but here's Vasya, look, Vasily Stepanovich! Why is he here? Do you understand anything at all?"

Nyusha turned and her eyes opened wide.

"My God," she exclaimed. "Why are you here? I sent him so he'd be in time to stop you. You missed each other!"

Shaibin and Vasya stood identically amazed as she wrung her slender hands. She had the courage to close Merichka's door and step out into the middle of the hallway but couldn't take her eyes off Vasya, as if she found everything about him painfully curious and painfully relevant to her. She went to her room and asked him to come in, and he silently obeyed, bowing his head to his chest, not knowing what to do with his hands.

When Shaibin heard the voices in Nyusha's room, he nearly ran away. Nyusha was speaking loudly, with an unusual firmness, and the sound of her voice now drove Alexei Ivanovich down the stairs.

"I should warn you that I was the one who sent Ilya Stepanovich away this morning," Nyusha said. "I had hopes he'd catch you, since you couldn't have received Adolf's telegram yet, the one sent last night in Ilya's name! Oh, Ilya will think I was the one who sent it, on purpose, to make it easier for Adolf to send you off to Russia!"

"I don't understand anything," Vasya said, irritated. "You know everyone—Ilya, Adolf, Alexei Ivanovich—but the telegram was from the day before yesterday and I received it as a matter of course. I don't think you and I have anything to talk about."

"He sent it on Saturday!" Nyusha exclaimed. "They used me to send Ilya Stepanovich away!"

"I'm leaving unless you tell me how you're involved."

"I don't have time to tell you who I am. Do you realize what it means to me if Ilya thinks I sent him away on purpose? That I'm in league with Kellerman?"

"No, I don't."

"Quiet! My God, how little like him you are. You have to go back right away, do you hear? I'll give you some money."

"Me, go back?" Vasya was stunned. "Are you in your right mind?"

He saw in Nyusha a crazy woman who in addition was meddling in other people's business.

"I am!" Nyusha exclaimed, flushing. "It's you who's not in his right mind, that's what! Where are you going? Do you know what Adolf is?"

"I'm going to Russia because I can't go on here anymore," Vasya said sullenly.

"And what's there?"

"Nothing. It's probably bad, but then there's less freedom. I don't know what to do with myself here."

Nyusha gazed at him and tears welled up in her eyes.

"Poor boy," she said. Vasya blushed, vexed. "A month ago I might have gone with you! You'll be lost there, that's what."

Vasya didn't answer. He sat down in the chair where Shaibin had sat the morning of the day before yesterday; there wasn't another in the room, actually. Nyusha came close, so close that her knees fit between his.

"Dear boy," she said with tears in her voice. "Don't go!"

He got scared that she was just about to touch

him with her soft hand, him, his coarse jacket faded under the arms, and see his perhaps not entirely clean neck.

"Dear boy," she repeated, "you don't have to go. Go back to your mama and Ilyusha. I know. There's no other road for you."

Vasya rudely pushed away from her.

"Leave me in peace!" he muttered. "What are you actually trying to do?" And he grinned.

She didn't take her eyes off him. She sat on the table and put her hand on his broad shoulder.

"There's no other road for you than entirely under Vera Kirillovna's wing," she said with anguish, and suddenly tears streamed down her face. "You don't even know why you're running away from her. I read your letters to Adolf, I dreamed about you, I thought, here's one more who might take me with him. But now—no! Listen. There's nowhere for you to run away from home to. I'll get you some money. Your mama's waiting for you."

She wept openly and didn't wipe away her tears. Vasya didn't know what to do and decided once again to try being rude.

"I think you could stop reading other people's letters. I'm not ten years old, to be scared by Vera Kirillovna . . . And you're being much too familiar."

"What's that? So be it! I'm scaring you? I'm talking to you the way Ilya might talk to me: Listen to me. Trust me. You can't?"

Vasya felt hot; he kept turning away from Nyusha over and over again.

"Whatever you want, I'll take care of everything," she said. "You won't see Adolf. I'll put you on the train tonight, I'll buy the ticket . . . Do you want me to kiss you?" she said very quietly and sadly all of a sudden, seeking his hand with hers. "Do you want to come to my room tonight?"

Tears were spilling from her eyes; she squeezed his fingers and looked shyly at him. At that moment Vasya felt his heart stop for a second. Where, where and when had he ever felt such gentle and cool fingers in his hand?

Possibly in a dream, a dream not that long ago, where Ilya's voice and the crackling of an envelope of tremendous importance had made him shudder with horror and shame. And then, exactly the same way, someone's small hand had caught his. Oh, how sweet, how wonderful that touch was! And how unmatchable it seemed!

He turned to face Nyusha, not knowing how to look into her eyes.

"Are you crying?" he said, just to say something in the confusion that was suffocating him. "I'd better go,

I'll come back later, a little later, when you've calmed down."

She let go of his hand. He stood up, but how could he leave like this, after what she'd said to him? Or did she have no shame at all?

She looked at him firmly, and her eyes were dry.

"Go, you're right," she said. "Go and think over what I said. Actually, you'll think about me even so."

She unlocked the door and he realized she was asking him to leave. Blushing thickly, so that only a narrow strip around his collar remained white, Vasya went out. After him, the smell of hay and tar, an unusual smell in the city, lingered in the room.

If he'd stayed one more minute, Nyusha would finally have had her usual fit of hysterics. But hysterics require an audience, humiliating though it is to admit, and Nyusha could only throw herself silently across the bed, tearing at her thin, light hair.

How, finally, could she vindicate herself in Ilya's eyes? She had only one option left: return Vasya to him no matter what. Her poor, helpless soul should be good for at least that. Yesterday, when she'd said a final goodbye to Adolf in their last telephone conversation, when, thinking to atone for her relationship with him, she'd betrayed him and sent Ilya away, she'd already realized that the one thing she did have to do was make sure Vasya remained. Not all was yet lost, or so it seemed to her. Oh, she would hold him back, she would follow him all the way to the station and run after the train, if necessary. After all, she had no one else left in the entire world.

Shaibin? But he was the same as herself. Once she'd told him just that: you're my soul mate. You're in the same pitch-dark I am. And that was the truth. She felt his alarm, his sufferings, as her own, and this alarm mounted, grew stronger and stronger with each passing day and utterly tortured her. When and by what means would the times Ilya predicted finally start?

For many of our secondary, and even tertiary heroes, this day proved far from idle. For instance, that day a telegram was received in Moscow (late in the day, most likely) saying that the younger Gorbatov had arrived safely in Paris and would continue on tomorrow.

As for Mr. Rastoropenko, both he and all his people (a total of thirty-two men and five women) had begun to pack up their goods and chattel, as the saying goes, and hastily gave up their jobs, whoever had one, so they could leave on Friday, as soon as the money and documents for their cut-rate passage arrived, so the money wouldn't be spent in vain. In those lands where they were supposed to go, or rather, close to those lands, and specifically on Ilya Gorbatov's farm, this Monday also proved not entirely tranquil. This day Marianna decided to have sewn not a blue dress for Christmas, but a white wedding dress, which later, in the spring, could be dyed—and Vera Kirillovna wholeheartedly agreed with her. Moreover, both of them, especially Vera Kirillovna, had focused their attention on the blind man, who had been brought at dinnertime on a wagon from L., battered and unconscious. In his delirium he twice mentioned Vasya and asked, in passing, why he still hadn't seen him. Anyuta wept until day's end, not leaving the old man's side, and the next day she was witness to things she'd never seen before. But we will have occasion to recount this a little later.

That day, Nyusha asked Merichka to stay with her. Vasya and his journey never left her thoughts. At the same time, she was afraid of being left alone, afraid of running into him. That was why she wouldn't let Merichka go: she was afraid he would come. At moments, she thought she should follow his every step; at others, she thought she shouldn't have anything to do with this rude, clumsy boy. There could be no question of seeing him in Merichka's presence, at least: Nyusha would burn from shame at Vasya's short jacket sleeves and sky-blue tie. When she recalled that unbearable heavenly color, she felt genuine rage toward Vasya.

Nonetheless, he was all she had left in the world, in the whole world where she lived and suffered. That night, when she returned home with Berta and Natasha, it seemed to her that going to his room, the sleeping man's room, and staying with him until morning would mean keeping him in Paris. But this method wasn't foolproof—she realized that—this method was the most shameful of all. She would never have the courage to admit it to Ilya. "Find a last among the lasts." That's what he'd told her once. But surely not by going to Vasya's room in the night and forcing him to stay by her side?

At the same hour the telegram was received in Moscow, Vasya was under the windows of the Kellerman apartment, hatless and coatless, on that elegant, deserted street we have already once described. The fact that Nyusha knew his, Vasya's, entire story in such detail, the fact that she was involved in his fate—the fate of some "young lout" (secretly, the word was even to his liking) leaving to join his father in Russia, with the help of a schoolmate—had aroused his curiosity from the first moment. This curiosity helped Vasya summon up the nerve to go see Kellerman. But he stood by the building across the way for nearly an hour (so that he could be easily seen, of course, from the windows of Mr. de R.'s former apartment), and when he finally entered the building, the doorman hastily announced that no one was home and there was no point in him going upstairs and troubling himself.

But why had he come, actually, and stood opposite this building? Deep down, his curiosity was gradually shifting to worry. One question arose there, as the sum total of all the conversations he had ever had with Ilya, a question born long ago, subconsciously, which Vasya had stifled due to the impossibility of answering it. Nyusha's appearance had forced him to consider it again. The question was this: Did anyone other than Stepan Vasilievich Gorbatov need Vasya Gorbatov? Could his departure really be important not only for him and his father but for other people he didn't know and didn't want to know?

He stayed up late that evening and heard Shaibin come in (he already knew they were neighbors), wash up, and toss and turn in bed for a long time. Then Vasya fell asleep, exhausted from a day spent aimlessly in the city. The maid woke him up: it was after noon. The young lady upstairs was asking whether the monsieur wouldn't like to come up for a minute. Vasya thought a moment and said he wouldn't. More than anything, he was afraid Nyusha would offer herself to him again—a notion he found utterly unbearable. Everything, everything, starting with his dream about her, was a secret he was already prepared to fight for (without even knowing Nyusha at all). He knew, he remembered always, that this could not come easily, otherwise there was no happiness. And all of a sudden she herself had summoned him, was giving herself to him. He closed his eyes; he grew cold. He was so ashamed he couldn't move.

He lay there until two or so and only then set out through the city. He stopped in at stores, twice ate a stale, sickly ham sandwich at a zinc counter. He came home before six, tired and dirty—he hadn't washed since the day before. Adolf walked into his room without knocking, like an older brother, like a boss.

There was now a patently undue familiarity to Adolf and the ease that comes from lots of easily earned money, expensive linen, and total impunity. He asked Vasya not to talk loudly at the train station; as always, there would be many detectives, and he didn't want to attract excessive attention. Vasya sat down on the bed. He wanted to find out from Adolf's eyes whether he knew Vasya had gone to see him yesterday. But Adolf's eyes were darting around.

"Tell me, shouldn't you write Father, telling him to meet me?" Vasya asked. The detectives had again reminded him of that old question that had been bothering him.

"Write? To what father?"

"Stepan Vasilievich. Or a telegram."

"Ah, yes! That will be done if you want."

No, those words told him nothing.

Vasya went out; Adolf led him. And so he was leaving without saying goodbye to Nyusha, though could she be the one who knew why he was going and who needed him? She knew too much! But shyness and awkwardness kept him from seeing her one more time.

Strange people surrounded Vasya's departure. A section of the train was going as far as Warsaw, the other right up to the border of the Russian state. "Negoreloye" was what was written on the train cars. In the first two classes, where Vasya was traveling, it was almost all Poles with superbly made luggage and languid, untalkative women who opened their boxes of sweets long before the train's departure. In third class, as always, the people were much more colorful. Traveling there, first, were two young Orthodox deacons who had tied up their pigtails and were rattling an enameled teapot by the window. They'd evidently come to Paris to visit someone and were now returning to their parish in some distant Polish district. There were a lot of women here; wearing scarves, primarily young, some nursing. Leisurely conversations had been struck up in anticipation of the night's journey.

Instead of luggage, Vasya had a small, very creaky basket, which looked incredibly pathetic on the shelf next to the Poles' grand hampers and traveling bags. Most of all, he was going to be freezing shortly after Berlin, if not before. With the money left over he had bought himself, besides this basket, also underwear and socks; nothing else had come to mind. He had about a hundred and fifty francs remaining, and he didn't know whether this would be enough for his ticket from the border to Moscow. The money was hidden in his old canvas purse.

Adolf kept checking the clock—to do this he had to walk a few steps away from the train—which hung over the door to the first-class waiting room; the heavy hand wouldn't move for a full minute and then in a single leap would jump to the next division on the giant clockface and shudder a few seconds more, as if recovering from the exertion.

There were quite a few people seeing others off. But was that what they were doing? Someone was scurrying about with a concerned look, running in his zeal all the way to the dining car, where in slender but sturdy vases transparent flowers were fading, where plates with outsize monograms gleamed, where the Italian waiter slipped a shiny French–Polish Bristol menu between glass and salt cellar.

Of these scurriers, one actually stopped too close to Adolf. He had neither a turned-up collar nor a hat pushed especially far back. He was an unremarkable person: in his right hand he was holding a small package, and if it hadn't been for his creaky shoes, Vasya wouldn't have noticed him at all.

Nyusha was running down the platform, as if afraid of not making it, although they had twenty-two minutes to go until the train's departure—Adolf had just checked the clock. This time her coat wasn't buttoned at all, and her short, wide dress was winding around her knees. Her umbrella was dripping—it was raining again in this autumnal city! She was running, peering at everyone standing by the cars, peering through the car windows, and her eyes were darting on her distraught, pale, suddenly unattractive face.

She noticed Adolf first; he was impossible not to notice. Many people had been glancing at his wide trousers. He was waving his bamboo cane and flashing his dark eyeglasses. She saw him and the thought that he would be witness to her possible victory made her head spin. She ran up to Vasya—who didn't recognize her in her street clothes.

"Why am I here?" she asked, possibly herself, possibly Vasya, panting. "Maybe inside you're laughing at me, Vasily Stepanovich? Last night you didn't come to my room, and it seemed too crude, too frank to go to yours. On the other hand, today you refused outright when I sent for you, and all day I didn't know what to think. And now, I'm here after all, and here I'm not ashamed to speak to you—especially in front of him"—and she indicated Adolf with her eyes. "I haven't come to see you off—you don't deserve that! I've come to take you away. Stop, don't interrupt!"

This she almost shouted at Adolf, who had managed to grab her above the elbow.

"Get out of here," he said, turning red. "You've lost your mind."

She jerked her shoulder and broke away from him. He left a mark on her famous rabbit fur coat—a scrap of the fine fur had torn off and fallen to the platform's asphalt.

"Oh, Lord, I guess this one's ready to fight! Do you know why I came running after you like a fool? I kept doubting, I doubted until the last minute, whether it was you, Vasily Stepanovich, who was the one who . . . No, I can't explain it to you right now, I'll tell you later. And all of a sudden something just stabbed me: it was you! And I forgot everything, forgot that you're nineteen and you have that awful blue tie that Merichka is going to laugh at. Listen to me!"

Vasya looked at her with an inexpressible feeling. His mouth was bone dry and half open.

"The reason Ilya left was to tell you, dear boy, that it does matter that you're going, and in life for the most part very few things do matter. Ilya rushed after you because he thought, as do I, that the telegram wouldn't arrive until Monday evening—he was the one who told me that, the scoundrel, he lied, and I believed him again." She pointed to Adolf with her whole arm, and he turned even redder than before, and he very obviously gave a sudden squeeze to the light cane in his (suede-gloved) hand. "Ilya rushed after you, but you turned out to be here. And you're going . . . where? To join who? Are you lying about your papa expecting you? Do you actually think he needs you?"

Adolf waved his cane a little, but not too much, so as not to draw the attention of others seeing people off, as if he were waving it as a joke, standing there and giving it a wave.

"Get out of here," he said again, and his lower lip jumped. "Everything you tell him is lies and filth."

Vasya stood in a kind of stupor. Another minute— he thought—and I'll learn everything, and for the first time in my life I'll be given the chance to be decisive, to be honest.

"Lies? Filth?" Nyusha whispered, and tears glittered in her eyes, but she wouldn't let them fall. "Vasily Stepanovich, this scoundrel is in the employ of your own father, the entire future of this shipbuilder is assured if you leave now. The money you were given, do you think your father sent it? Stop! There is no Stepan Vasilievich Gorbatov!"

Vasya rushed to her.

"What are you saying? That can't be!" he cried out, catching her hand.

"En voitures!" came the call from far away, near the baggage car. "En voitures! En voitures!" kept being repeated, closer and closer still. The heavy doors were slamming.

Adolf didn't move. What was happening in his eyes, behind the dark glass, no one could see.

"Well, enough of this," he said distinctly. "Get in the car or else your basket will leave."

Vasya turned his contorted face to him. He had collected his whole self in an emotional effort hitherto unknown to him. The moment was so vivid, so sharp, it spilled out into three words that he nearly shouted at the top of his lungs: I am alive!

What was happening inside him—he had no name

for it, he didn't even try to find the right words to express what was burning his soul. He mastered this difficult, this happy inspiration and his face regained its only slightly agitated appearance. He saw Nyusha, and the fact that tears were streaming down her face, and the fact that they were falling on her hands. And it felt impossible to ask again about anything.

"Get me out of here," he told her.

A door clanged shut behind him, and a long whistle that set red circles spinning in front of him trembled in the air. The wheels started turning.

A ponderous brass band quickly tuned up—and its musicians quickly lined up. In each window someone waved a white handkerchief, and someone responded to each. The train cars, shuddering, gradually found their rhythm in the overarching melody.

The train sped past the depot with a wild buzzing at the switches; it whistled one last time and sobbed a long, wobbling howl. And in the gloom, damp and autumnal, above the dull rails, a small red light stayed on for a long minute.

Adolf stood exactly as long as everyone else did. He watched the train go with everyone else, until its trace was lost among a dozen other lights, red, green, and yellow. Next to them, a train newly arrived from Calais howled, and its iron carriages clattered.

When everyone started for the exit, so did Adolf, so as not to lag behind the others under any circumstance. He tried to walk in step with the people next to him, but his whole back felt someone's gaze. He felt it with the back of his head, his shoulders, his waist, as if he were being stabbed; he made a tremendous effort not to speed up. He walked down the wide corridor and stairs with a studied nonchalance and came out on the square. He immediately saw Nyusha and Vasya finally finding a cab—the Calais passengers had snapped them all up, the weather playing its part—and getting in and the driver lazily lowering the meter. And at that very minute, whoever it was stopped looking at Adolf's back: next to him, shoes creaked, and the man with the package, shaking his head and winking simultaneously, ran through the puddles toward the Métro.

The cab pulled away from the station and turned into the street, and the windows immediately fogged up from the rain. Inside there was dusk, humidity, gasoline. From time to time, the broad, swift beam of an oncoming headlight lashed through the dusk and at the same time ran across Nyusha, her open neck, her hands, and even her light stockings.

Without looking, Vasya sensed the lights slipping over her, and the temptation to see her, to look straight at her, became irresistible. This temptation held so much genuine bliss that at first he slowly shifted his eyes to her small feet pressed closely together, to her knees swathed in her short coat, to her hands in their rabbit skin gloves. He held back for a few long, infinitely happy seconds somewhere near her open collar, between her checkered scarf, the shadow of her dress, and her delicate neck, and finally looked into her face.

"Kiss me," he said suddenly, surprising himself, dying from fear and cautiously touching her torn sleeve with his finger.

She turned to him and looked at him, surprised and stern.

"Do you know how to work? What can you do?"

He did not take his light, shining eyes off her.

"I'm asking you. What do you intend to do? You have to find a job tomorrow."

"I will. I'll go to the factory. We'll move out of your hotel"—and he caught his breath.

Now they were waiting at an intersection under a policeman's baton.

"Kiss me," he said again, forgetting himself, "look at me."

He didn't know what he should do. He reached out and practically scorched himself when he touched her glove.

"This evening you're going to find different rooms. I'll tell you where to look."

"A different room."

He moved his knees toward her knees—and suddenly felt that no more words should be spoken. Out of a sense of contradiction and outrageous confusion he also said, "Take off your glove."

"Take it off yourself," she said very quietly.

He still had his arms around her when the cab stopped at the hotel entrance.

The staircase took a sharp turn to the left toward the first floor. Nyusha knew every wrinkle in the dusty carpet, every spot on the shabby runner. A sconce lit the staircase with an intensely red light that left the sign telling people to wipe their feet in shadow. Alexei Ivanovich Shaibin was coming down the stairs slowly, practically groping. It was dinnertime. He was wearing a hat and a—deplorable-looking—raincoat. His face, under a brim somewhat wider than usual, was distracted, and he walked straight toward Vasya, holding the railing tight—such was his habit.

His face was hard to make out under the hat brim and in the lamp's meager light, but his entire tall, still quite slender figure, despite his slightly rounded shoulders expressed an indifference to everything around him and a focus on himself. Indeed, after sitting for an hour over a map of Paris (God knows where he had obtained that old map, transparent at the folds), he had the right to an expression like this.

He raised his hat—and this courtesy again held something new and even haughty. This time he recognized Vasya as soon as he saw him. Nyusha was still below.

"I thought you were planning to go somewhere today, weren't you?" Shaibin asked with supreme restraint. "Or did you change your mind?"

Vasya walked past him and suddenly blushed.

"No, you were mistaken," he said, flustered. "I'm not going anywhere."

At that moment, Shaibin's eyes met Nyusha's, which stunned him. He saw her different, completely new, a stranger, with a tearstained face (she had never wept in his presence), and with lips from which the rouge had helplessly come off. He had the feeling she wanted to give him some sign. She raised her eyebrows and quickly pointed out Vasya to him. She didn't want to say, Be quiet! Don't ask questions! But at the same time, her look seemed to be inviting Alexei Ivanovich to be in on something with her.

He stepped aside. She walked past.

He pulled his hat over his eyes and grabbed the railing again. She had brought him back—the first clear thought in a long time passed through him. Now the time has finally come to follow through with the rest.

Lost in thought, he went outside.

A cab was already parked at the entrance. The driver was in no hurry; it was raining harder and harder. Shaibin opened the door (oh, he still had some money left!). He breathed in the traces of Nyusha's perfume; this was her farewell to him! And pulling the scrap of newspaper out of his jacket pocket and slowly dealing with the door so that, God forbid, he didn't hit anyone walking down the sidewalk, he read out Mr. Rastoropenko's address to the driver.

The cab drove readily away from the entrance, and since the street was too narrow to turn around, they had to go a little farther, six or so buildings, in the direction of the cemetery, and only then turned down-hill, toward the broad boulevard.

CHAPTER EIGHT

As soon as it started growing light and half the sky was pink, Marianna pushed the barn door open with her knee and went into the yard. The roosters were crowing nonstop. She ran her hand over her face, which was as sleepy and grumpy as a child's, and looked around. The attic was closed. Just as she'd thought! Ilya was back, so it was good she hadn't slept in Vasya's bed last night.

This time she couldn't even stretch out on the floor, next to Vera Kirillovna, as she had that night Shaibin spent with them. They'd put Anyuta on the floor and moved Marianna's bed back into the kitchen, where the blind wayfarer had coughed and moaned all night and prayed feverishly in his muffled, sobbing voice.

In the barn, Marianna was plagued by fleas; she slept on the hay, and although Vera Kirillovna did say that in her distant youth, in Novgorod Province, she'd had to spend more than one night in the hayloft, while still a student, Marianna was not happy: the alfalfa was half mixed with straw, and the straw cut into Marianna's legs and chest; in the middle of the night she'd had to put clothes on and sleep in her dress.

She went over to the spigot in the yard, let go a solid stream and, pedaling back until the stagnant water flushed out, stripped naked and used the small dipper hanging there to drench herself from head to toe. She dried off in the wind, threw on her chemise, dress, and apron, and wrapping her head in a clean kerchief (she'd left her straw hat in the house the previous night), proceeded to the chickens.

The chickens were waking up, the sun was rising. Marianna absentmindedly scattered a handful of grain for them at the henhouse entrance, and the dog circled around her—it knew she was about to go to the cows. Marianna rinsed the milk pail—there were three milk cows.

They were crowded in the humid, dark warmth. A calf pressed up to the belly of its reddish spotted mother. Marianna pulled on her teats and the milk frothed. Far away, from the direction of the old farm, she heard the herder's long horn.

The herd was coming from far off, collecting the livestock from the farms as it went. Two dogs, a male and a bitch, followed dejectedly under the tails of the last cows, while twenty paces away the herder played majestically, newspaper in hand.

Ilya saw the cows go out and saw Marianna, her head tilted back and her arms spread slightly, watch them go, until the herder and the newspaper in his hand were out of sight. Ilya went downstairs, washed, drank some milk, and ate some of the bread Marianna brought from the kitchen. They talked about this and that, about Vasya, about Monsieur Jolifleur . . . Not a word about the lilac soap. Marianna proceeded to the vegetable garden.

Here, finally, she had to complete the work begun back on Thursday with Vasya. The cabbage they'd planted that summer had to be transplanted all over again; she needed to weed the cauliflower and, despite yesterday's rain, water it again, while the sun was still low; moreover, it was time to plant spinach and celeriac and harvest the late beets and carrots and the last, heavy tomatoes bursting ripe.

In a week, or about that, Marianna would have to start turning over a good half of the garden. In a week, the great labors were supposed to begin for the most part. Ilya would go out for the first time onto his own field to sow wheat. He would go out with his own grain, purchased long ago, one hundred sixty kilograms for one hectare, and he would sow it by hand, even though his former boss had offered him his sowing machine, like last year, when Ilya was still a sharecropper and sowed oats for him. He'd sown oats not here but next to this; this strip was usually a potato field. Now, though, next August, Ilya would have his own wheat. He said that in all likelihood he would harvest it himself—twenty kilograms—and would also reap five thousand of straw per hectare. The sort of wheat Ilya had selected, as it happens, was called Bon Fermier.

Marianna spent a few hours working on the beds. Ilya had long since harnessed the oxen, loaded the cart with pungent, friable manure, and left for the field. In the house, the windows had gradually opened, and Anyuta had gone out on the porch, teary and taciturn. Vera Kirillovna brought in the firewood, heated the stove, and checked on the chickens; then she brought a pail out from under the porch, and, seeing Marianna's black dress in the garden, mixed the hogs' slop herself.

By now the sun was high. The day was beginning in the gold and sparkle Marianna was used to. A couple of times she went down for water and rattled the dipper at the spigot. Finally, a distinct impatience appeared on her face. She dropped everything and quietly, right under the windows, went behind the temporary pigsty, which had been knocked together from boards. (The pigs were crowded there and were always making noise; "We have such badly behaved pigs," Marianna had said then.)

Behind the pigsty, standing tall and perfectly still, was Gabriel.

"You're here? Why didn't you say something?" Marianna was offended.

"I was afraid, afraid of bothering you," he mumbled shyly.

"What's the matter with you?"

She looked at him with glittering eyes.

"You're my fiancée now . . ."

For a minute they couldn't tear themselves away from each other, she hung completely on his neck.

"Why didn't you come yesterday?" Marianna asked, gasping. "You deceiver, you."

"I couldn't. They took me to the tailor's. Marianna, the wedding's soon!"

"Not before January. That's what we decided on Sunday."

He held her close again, squashing her nose against his fresh, cool cheek.

"But until then?"

"What until then?"

He turned red, looked away, and suddenly saw Ilya's jacket on the porch.

"Ilya's back? Where is he?"

He released Marianna, and she laughed so loudly that she had to cover her mouth with her hand.

"Where is he? Why are you laughing, silly girl?"

Marianna bent over double from laughter.

"Who are you marrying, me or him? In the field, the field, with the oxen, and the manure . . ."

He stood perplexed for a few moments and waited for her to finish laughing. She stopped abruptly and glanced in fright around the pigsty, making sure there was no one nearby.

"Listen," she said in a rapid whisper. "I'll come to the grove tonight, but only if there's no moon, understand? Don't just stand there as if I'd already come, hold me! I'm not coming because you want it but because I do."

She hugged him close once more and ran off.

He stood there a little longer, and the pigs scampered behind the wooden barrier. Then his heart began beating more evenly and his breath came less noisily. He cautiously walked out toward the big maple on the boundary strip; it seemed to him the height of indecency to let Vera Kirillovna set eyes on him. There he thought for a minute, seeing nothing around, and then he pulled himself together, made a visor of his hand, stared into the distance, and confidently walked toward the recently plowed potato field. When he saw

Ilya from far off, he once again felt such a surge of happiness that it took all his strength to keep from running toward him.

In Vera Kirillovna's house, meanwhile, on the stool by the stove, Anyuta was laundering her colorful skirt. She was wearing Marianna's chemise, which fell to her heels. She cautiously ran her fingers through the soapy foam. She had her hair in two braids—the way Vera Kirillovna had plaited it; her bare feet were pink now, not black, and her large, troubled eyes would fill with tears and then sparkle with delight and amazement. From time to time she would cast her shining gaze at the far corner where the blind man lay on his back, his hands resting on top of the flannelette blanket, his shirt unbuttoned so anyone could see the two scars along his left clavicle and the two white spots on his dark, sunken chest.

"Granddad, why don't I call a doctor for you?" Anyuta whispered clearly. "Why don't I, dear Granddad? You'll be better in no time."

The blind man moved his hand and parted his cracked lips.

"I'd like a little water," he said softly but distinctly. Anyuta handed him the mug by his side.

"Is it you, little one?" he said barely audibly. "I'll be going away soon."

Anyuta leaned all the way over him, her hands pressed to her chest.

"And I'll go with you, Granddad," she said with tears in her voice.

"No, I'm going alone. You'll stay here."

In the dimly lit kitchen the fire could be heard crackling hotly under the burner.

"When will I see Ilyusha?" the wayfarer asked, as if he might actually see him. "I wish they would show me Ilyusha."

At that moment Vera Kirillovna walked in.

She was the same as ever. Neither Vasya's flight nor Shaibin's silence could take away the main thing about her face: the stamp of a beautiful and unwavering serenity. Her sleeves were rolled up, her hair combed smooth and gathered into a braid.

She walked silently to the head of the wayfarer's bed.

"Wouldn't you like something?" she asked, more gently than any whisper. "Do you want some black coffee or a little wine in your water?"

But the wayfarer dropped back into oblivion. This time he didn't rave but merely let out a long moan from deep in his chest. The right side of his chest obviously hurt because he kept touching it. All day, his eyes remained at half mast and his whole face took on a sickly cast.

Occasionally, for the brief moments when he seemed to return to consciousness, barely folding his fingers, he made the cross around him and then over himself, barely moving his lips. He seemed to be gradually losing his hearing; in any case, noises and voices had ceased to trouble him altogether. Even when Vera Kirillovna, Ilya, Marianna, and Anyuta were having dinner—in total silence—he paid them no attention whatsoever. His hands were swollen and darker, and Marianna tried not to look at them.

But in the evening, when a narrow, coppery strip of sky reached the kitchen window and then suddenly, as if they had vanished in an instant, the birds in the henhouse fell silent, he came around.

Ilya was alone in the kitchen at the time. His elbows leaning on the table and his round head propped on both hands, he sat in a deep and drowsy reverie. The cows were back, Marianna and Anyuta had milked them, and Vera Kirillovna was still sorting out the plums; she had filled an entire basket with thirty kilos of them and had decided to take them to town tomorrow—market day. Ilya was sitting at the table and suddenly felt he wasn't alone, as can happen when a person sleeping in the room with you wakes up.

"Ilyusha, is that you?" the wayfarer asked, moving his hand. His scar, almost black, was barely visible in the dusk. "I'm about to die, Ilyusha, and I haven't taken communion, I want to confess to you."

Ilya recoiled from the table.

"No, no, I'm not worthy. What are you saying!"

"Understand, my friend, if I'm going to die a sinner, unforgiven, at least let my soul unburden itself—let it open up to you. Listen to me. No priest would ever give me communion. I haven't forgiven my enemies, I haven't loved those who are far away, I haven't forgiven the evildoers, I can't forgive! I've been cruel . . . Since the war it's been."

Full of trepidation, Ilya didn't take his eyes off the wayfarer.

"How can I forgive them anyway, Ilyusha? God himself, in his power and glory, could not forgive them for what they've done! And pray for them? Call their actions mistakes? No!"

With great difficulty, he rose up on the pillows, his sickly beard fell to one side, and his blind eyes were wide open.

"The Son of Man, Jesus Christ, Who forgave the robber, wouldn't forgive them, He'd consign them to the fire and Hell, I'm telling you. But what He, all-wise, can do, is not permitted me, a sinner, who was given the commandments to love and not kill. I didn't love, I hated, and I hate to this day. And I killed."

His head dropped to his chest.

"How can I forgive? There is no forgiveness in me, no prayer for them, Ilyusha! I'm hard with people. By what right? the Angel will ask me. I wasn't thinking about my right, I'll tell Him, but I swear, oh, Lord, I swear to you—pride is not the reason for my hatred!"

He no longer felt the chest pain that had wracked him for two days—or did he feel a different, stronger pain rending his soul?

"It is God's decree—we are in a foreign land. Separated, overtaken by suffering. But even here, what do we see around us? Once again, people know not what they do. They were given reason—but where is their reason? They were called, but they destroy both themselves and others ... We must forget frivolous thoughts and remember the children. Even Shaibin I can't forgive. How can he redeem his guilt before Anyuta? If not for him, her father might not have died, and her mother's sister would not have come to the life he led her to, and her mother herself! What did she die for? For his frivolous love. I can't forgive him!"

Ilya was pale. Drops of sweat were running slowly down his face.

"Shaibin will atone," he said flatly, "I plead for Shaibin. He will atone for everything. He has admitted his responsibility."

The blind man turned his dark face toward Ilya.

"He'll reckon with God. I can't forgive frivolity in life. I love the difficulty of life, the difficulty of life, Ilyusha. You, acknowledge your fate, overcome your fate. Lord have mercy on this sinner!"

For a long time he didn't say anything. Ilya was afraid to move.

"So much for commandments," the wayfarer whispered softly, "and so much for atonement! I'm a sinner, Ilyusha, a great sinner. Will you pray for me?"

For the first time a mysterious question flashed through Ilya's mind.

"Who am I to pray for? Tell me. Your name?"

But the wayfarer didn't answer. He fell back on his pillow again and lay silently for a while, not moving. The light was fading, the sky's copper strip was gone, and a brief, strong wind had come up.

"Will they be here?" the blind man asked, breathing heavily.

"Yes."

And indeed, a few minutes later Marianna and Anyuta walked into the house, and then so did Vera Kirillovna.

"Have them sit down. I want to sing for them."

Anyuta had never seen him so debilitated. She was used to listening to him sing in the open air, on the road.

Vera Kirillovna said, "Better he sleep. This is no time for singing!"

But the wayfarer called Ilya over and with his help sat up on the bed. He folded his hands, as for prayer, lowered his head, and took a minute to recover from the exertion, which caused him deep pain, then suddenly lifted his head. His face was unrecognizable.

"I will sing you what I promised. Remember, I stopped by to see you last week? Remember, we were interrupted? I wanted to sing you a certain song, I sang it outside Toulouse with the Cossacks, and I also sang it on our journey, isn't that right, Anyuta? I won't be singing anymore, so let this one, let this song stay with you. This is my legacy—this and Anyuta."

He inhaled with his entire sick chest, rolled his white eyes, and cautiously began in a quivering voice, high but true:

> Grieve not, Cossack, in this strange country,
> Yearn not, Cossack, for Russia-Russia,
> Were you not given freedom so free,
> A path, a way across the earth?
> Walk that path, that way, all round,
> 'Til you come to the land of the French.
> Make a stand, a home, on a mountain steep,
> Lay a boundary, a circle 'round your little field!

Mourn not, Cossack, in this strange country,
For your father's grave, your mother's,
Be strong, Cossack, in your destiny,
In your land, so very far away.

(This song was recorded in September 1928, to the west of Muret.)

Marianna remained seated for a minute, her hands dropped to her slightly parted knees. The cracked voice sent a shudder through her. Pressing a hand to her face, palm out, she leapt up and backed toward Vera Kirillovna.

"But he left. Mama! He ran away in the night, like a thief!" she cried in a voice full of tears. She hid her face and rushed toward the door in confusion.

The wayfarer slowly held his hands out to her and immediately dropped them. He had no strength left. Ilya rushed to him, laid him down, and covered up his large, skinny body as best he could. The dying man's breath became agonizing and rapid, as if he were grasping for breath with his lips; Vera Kirillovna lit a lamp, and in its light his entire face looked like the bark of a dark, hundred-year-old tree. Ilya saw sweat and tears running down that tough bark.

"Lord, accept Your slave Yakov," Ilya caught the blind man's whisper.

Time and again he brought his tensely trembling hands to his mouth and nose, doing this unconsciously, as if he were trying to brush away loose, greasy dirt in there. This was the end. No more than two hours passed in Ilya and Vera Kirillovna's silent tending. The end came to this strange man in gasps, in moans, in the final dark foam that appeared on his lips.

He now lay stretched out, his large hands bound at his chest, covered with an old Gorbatov blanket, his bare feet poking out. A two-sou coin was placed in each of his sunken eye sockets, and Ilya took a lantern into the yard to hew a coffin. Here lay the boards Gabriel had prepared for the new flooring, but they would do for a coffin too, he just had to make them fit. The first thing is to know a trade. Who had said that to him recently? Oh, he'd learned to be a joiner and a carpenter. Now he'd be a coffin-maker.

The lantern flickered in the wind, which was strong and warm, and the stars would come out and then hide in the clouds. The moon wasn't due to rise until late that night, and near dawn, by all accounts, there would be a strong, massive rain.

Ilya hammered and sawed.

"Why are you crying, Anyuta?" Vera Kirillovna said. "You're not alone, you'll stay with us. You'll be

Marianna's helper, all right? Won't you be loved here the way Granddad loved you?"

"That's just how my Papa lay," Anyuta whispered through her tears, pointing to the corpse.

They talked for a long time. Marianna never did return to the house. She quietly went to bed in her old place, in the fragrant alfalfa. But she was smarter now: she didn't undress at all. She lay in the darkness and thought.

She couldn't stop. Neither the late hour, nor her weariness, nor, finally, the blows of the hammer, could cut short the long, unspoken conversation she was having in her imagination with Vasya. Her eyes were open, and her arms, as was her constant habit, were flung wide. She was saying amazing things to herself, words that burned right through her, and Vasya was answering her. It went on like this for quite a while. The light in the yard went out and Ilya went up to his room. Still she couldn't stop, her face was burning, her heart was pounding; nothing like this had ever happened to her.

Ilya went up to his room. He would have to live in toil and sweat for several days and in uneasy sleep for several nights, until he could finally see with his own eyes the fruits of his efforts: the Rastoropenko party was expected in town on Saturday. This time, Ilya would not be able to explain anything to his friend, the

Advocate. Even he didn't understand what hopes, what worries he had brought with him from distant Paris.

He was used to acting almost without thinking. He'd never had any interest in "catching" people. For him, the life of Russians abroad was one unending disaster. He was grabbing people by the hands and feet as if they were drowning. He was rushing after them as if they were on fire. Nothing could stop him from doing this: not the temptation that Nyusha was for him, as great as it was, nor her infatuation. Nor was anyone capable of easing this task for him. Vera Kirillovna's entire love for Alexei Ivanovich had expressed itself only in her tacit, secret agreement with Ilya's intentions, which had come to Ilya from out of nowhere— out of the unsettled air that people breathe in exile.

Vera Kirillovna's love for Alexei Ivanovich had forced her to join forces with Ilya. Her disingenuous summoning of Shaibin from Africa, her conversation with the man, full of sincerity and affection, and even her tears, which he took to Paris on his face—all of it promised him that vague but forever justified liberty he had striven toward and run away from his whole life. She told him she didn't love him, and it was true, she no longer loved him the way she once had—for herself, in herself, herself in him. Now she had given up everything for his peace of mind, now a new and honest period had come in her imperfectly understood love for him. What had she done to give herself to him like this? She hadn't had to do anything, merely pass with the light tread of imperishable memory through her own past. To embody this power of her own humiliation, she had only had to say a few words, glance a few times, take a deep breath, and run her roughened hand through his thick, heavy hair. Ilya had done the rest. Now all Vera Kirillovna had to do was accept Alexei Ivanovich as she had dreamed of seeing him. Had she known something? Guessed something? Had she secretly waited, with Ilya, for news of the Paris party? Or had she merely in her own way not let Shaibin go from her memory?

At about five o'clock in the evening, on Saturday, the day after the blind man's funeral, at an hour when Ilya was in the field, an hour when he could not be at home, Alexei Ivanovich Shaibin showed up at the Gorbatov farm's vegetable garden.

He no longer looked like a "man from Africa." For one thing, he did not come from town on foot, like that other time, when he got so tired of looking into the distance, searching in that distance for the Gorbatov plane trees he'd been told about in town. He took a bus to the crossroads memorable to him for a certain reason and only then set off on foot.

He walked neither slowly nor quickly. The day was clean and bright. At the little bridge that led to the old farm, he hesitated. He tried to look past the rows of crooked apple trees in order to see at least a part of the life that faced him: the straw hat, the shovel in his rough hand, the black clumps of greasy dug-up earth ... After passing the first plane trees, which rustled drowsily at him, he saw smoke over the roof, transparent, an especially clean smoke, blue like the sky and curled like a cloud. He walked up to the gate.

Someone might have seen him from the kitchen window, but he didn't notice anyone. He stood there for rather a long time, he was in no rush to get anywhere. He was standing at his goal. Finally, someone walked through the yard, a woman. It might have been either Marianna or Vera Kirillovna.

The woman saw Alexei Ivanovich from afar and dropped her glittering white basin, which rolled with a clang at her feet. The woman didn't even pick it up; she started for the gate with a swift and almost inaudible step—that's how light it was; every second, Shaibin saw Vera Kirillovna's clear, pale, slightly wan face, her eyebrows and eyes, and the two bright spots on her cheeks.

"Come in. Why are you standing there like that?" she said, reaching for the latch.

He saw the small black cracks on her long, even fingers, the dark gold wedding ring, and another, an old silver ring that had lost all its turquoise over the years; he saw the big—no, huge—safety pin that fastened her apron at her chest, still so even, still so high; then he saw the fabric buttons at her dress collar, incongruous buttons, and the crude, ancient chain of her cross.

"Vera, be surprised for me, surprised at my return, laugh at me, otherwise it's going to be too hard, too embarrassing for me with you," Shaibin said, and his eyes suddenly became moist and tense. She shook her head.

"You're back and that's that," she said quietly. "Don't ask too much of me."

He followed her into the orchard where, a little more than a week before, he'd felt his head spin so powerfully. So this is how they'd lived! Right in front of the house, two roosters were fighting—one young, one old—so that the sand was flying in all directions; some child's shoes (you mean they had children?) lay white in the sun.

Shaibin took off his hat and sat down on the porch step, on the warm, stone step traced with chicken shit.

"This time, Vera, I'm here for good, as Marianna says. My Paris is over. Ilya has dealt with my life."

She sat facing him on the low bench put there for no particular reason.

"Whether it's Ilya or you, there's no way for me to know, and I don't have to. Now I'm with you—a stone around your neck. You won't untie me."

She smiled, and wrinkles appeared on both her cheeks, wrinkles she'd had since youth and that Marianna called dimples.

"A stone around your neck," she repeated. "Vasya's place is free."

Her smile again made his eyes glitter intensely.

"You've misunderstood me," he said, like a young man. "Oh, my God, I've said something terribly foolish. I've come here with the whole party, and Rastoropenko has already found me work."

She sat up straight.

"You've come with them all, Alyosha? So not to the 'lap of nature' and not 'with a softened heart'?"

She couldn't help herself and laughed quietly and briefly, and her hands, which had been folded in her lap, dropped to her sides.

"And you know what kind of work he found me? You'll never believe it. Bookkeeping!"

She raised her eyebrows and half opened her mouth—every word of his was like a song for her, clouding her mind and filling her soul with joy.

"You want me to tell you how it all happened? It wasn't all that simple, and I was afraid he wouldn't take me along. When I went to see Rastoropenko, he looked at me as if I were a perfect villain. Where had I come from? What was this? (It was Ilya who'd left me the address.)"

"Ilya? So he knew you were coming?"

"Oh, no. Otherwise he would certainly have told you so. He left me the address 'just in case.' The hell if I know what that meant to him, since he says he's acting 'without hope'. . . . So you see, Mr. Rastoropenko (an extremely busy person, I'll tell you, these days it's fashionable to depict people like that in literature), this gentleman simply showed me the door. And then it occurred me to go for help to a certain good person who was once quite active with respect to revolutions and who now is especially fine because he's retired. I knew he was involved in all sorts of philanthropy, and I also knew he knew Ilya, but it turned out he knew Rastoropenko as well—everyone in Paris knows each other, you wouldn't believe it. This good man immediately took me back to see Rastoropenko and said he vouched for me and even loaned me a little money. Truth be told, I'd had a terrible time of it in Paris. But even that worked out and I ended up not needing his money. The night before departure, three in the party decided not to go, they said they'd got a job at Delage and they preferred to stay. Rastoropenko said there

was something fishy about that, but I didn't understand what he was implying. In short, they took me
instead of one of those staying, and I came at official
expense, I've just signed a contract, and they even
insured me. But out of respect for my gray hair"—he
smiled, pausing for a few seconds—"they decided to
make something more senior out of me. My degree
and all that, they said . . . On top of that, my lameness. There, outside town, they've got an enormous
business, Vera, they're proposing nearly doubling the
asparagus canning factory, but they won't take Russian
workers for the factory. The Russians are being used
for the asparagus itself. But that's all they need. For all
of them this is just the start of a stable life of their
own."

Vera Kirillovna sat and listened. Here he was
explaining to her! Where did he get the audacity! She
smiled and immediately became attentive again.

"I'm telling you all this with a certain lightness, a
levity even," Shaibin said. "Ilya taught me that.
Weren't you the one who said to either do what I did
or perish? You were the one who said that otherwise it
was the noose. Vera, you were right . . ."

Vera Kirillovna listened intently to every word.
Despite his even voice and joyful face, he had
changed over their brief separation, couldn't help

but change, couldn't help but suffer in the capital, and the traces of those sufferings were everywhere, even in his too distinctly shiny gray hair. She sensed a surge in him, the kind that comes after a decision taken, and she knew that after this surge would come exhaustion, disappointment perhaps, regret perhaps. And then that, too, would pass. Beyond him, beyond the outlines of the shoulders and somewhat narrow head she held dear, she saw his life. And at that moment, the past seemed to cease to exist altogether. Now the direct opposite of the past was beginning. A future was beginning in which she had become mistress.

"I have to go, I don't want to get back too late," Shaibin said.

"You won't stay for supper?"

He refused. He already saw himself on the way back, saw the fields, the plane trees . . .

He stood up, and the Gorbatov yard with the nervous chickens and the sluggish shaggy dog suddenly reminded him that he had not come here to boast at all but to finish Vasya's story.

"He hasn't written you since he left?" Shaibin asked, and Vera Kirillovna immediately guessed who he meant.

"No, and he won't."

"That's true, he won't. I saw him. He didn't go to Moscow, he stayed in Paris. He was brought back from the train station."

"He didn't leave?" Vera Kirillovna repeated. "What are you saying! You're mistaken! Who could have brought him back?"

"I'm telling you: he was brought back. That evening he left the hotel where we were staying, and I don't know his address. It was she who brought him back. People say his luggage went, but whether or not he had luggage, I don't know. She moved with him."

"And who is this person?"

"You don't know her . . . She dragged him straight from the train—that's what her girlfriends said, and now she won't let him out of her sight. I saw them that very evening."

"But who is she?"

Shaibin didn't look at Vera Kirillovna. He looked to the side, maybe toward the road, where a tall wagon was speeding by just then; the whip was circling in the sky, the wheels rumbling.

"You don't know her," he said emphatically. "Ilya does. Tell him her name is Anna Martynovna Slyotova."

He glanced at her again but did not reach out. She stood there distraught, not knowing what to think. Did she or didn't she dare rejoice in what he'd said? Did his words mean joy or sorrow? "Joy, joy," she whispered to herself. Or was the joy in that it was Shaibin who had spoken these words?

She folded her arms.

"Alyosha," she said softly—"No, it's nothing, forgive me! . . . So you know for certain that Vasya is in Paris?"

"For certain."

"Well, thank you. That is a great consolation to me, after all, and to Marianna and Ilya. Thank you for coming, for telling me."

He started back toward the gate. He was walking and thinking, thinking with his heart, Here one life ends and another begins. Here is the vertical line dividing my time in half. I've done everything, said everything. Oh, my conscience!

He went out of sight behind a large, unruly currant bush; the orchard was quiet. The peach trees whispered in the sunset's breathing, only the cypresses were still and majestic, the ones just before the fields began, before the meadow, forest, and open expanses began . . .

Vera Kirillovna stood there looking straight ahead. The axe leaning against the porch gleamed in the sun like a piece of mirror. Finally, she closed her eyes— and that piece of blinding mirror, that piece of sun, became a black spot.

First it widened, obscuring the sparks falling up, and then started to look like an enormous jellyfish; then it narrowed to a point—and the sparks stopped falling, floating in place, trembling, changing color; while they shone, the point was black, and when they faded, so did the point. And the red sky where all this was happening gradually turned to gray, and the gold and black stars dwindled, moving off to the side.

When Vera Kirillovna opened her eyes, Anyuta emerged from the garden holding the watering can. She, too, had started wearing a round straw hat (Marianna had given her her old one). Anyuta walked over to the spigot, solemnly brought the watering can up to it, and waited for the watering can to fill. Then she firmly turned the spigot with both hands and started back, pulled to one side by the weight and holding her arm out exaggeratedly far (the way Marianna did). A few heavy drops fell on her dusty wooden shoe.

1928–29, Provence—Paris.

STEFAN ZWEIG · EDGAR ALLAN POE · ISAAC BABEL
TOMÁS GONZÁLEZ · ULRICH PLENZDORF · JOSEPH KESSEL
VELIBOR ČOLIĆ · LOUISE DE VILMORIN · MARCEL AYMÉ
ALEXANDER PUSHKIN · MAXIM BILLER · JULIEN GRACQ
BROTHERS GRIMM · HUGO VON HOFMANNSTHAL
GEORGE SAND · PHILIPPE BEAUSSANT · IVÁN REPILA
E.T.A. HOFFMANN · ALEXANDER LERNET-HOLENIA
YASUSHI INOUE · HENRY JAMES · FRIEDRICH TORBERG
ARTHUR SCHNITZLER · ANTOINE DE SAINT-EXUPÉRY
MACHI TAWARA · GAITO GAZDANOV · HERMANN HESSE
LOUIS COUPERUS · JAN JACOB SLAUERHOFF
PAUL MORAND · MARK TWAIN · PAUL FOURNEL
ANTAL SZERB · JONA OBERSKI · MEDARDO FRAILE
HÉCTOR ABAD · PETER HANDKE · ERNST WEISS
PENELOPE DELTA · RAYMOND RADIGUET · PETR KRÁL
ITALO SVEVO · RÉGIS DEBRAY · BRUNO SCHULZ · TEFFI
EGON HOSTOVSKÝ · JOHANNES URZIDIL · JÓZEF WITTLIN